As the head enforcer for the Shifter Council, Mycroft Portent doesn't usually do field work. Except, with Fate blessing those under him with finding mates and taking unexpected leave, he finds himself shorthanded. When a report of a shifter alpha shirking his duties to his pride comes across his desk, he decides to head to Texas himself, taking fellow enforcer Dakota Drudeson with him.

Tailing several members of the pride's inner circle leads Mycroft to a backwater honky-tonk bar. He and Dakota head inside, intending to watch their behavior. Mycroft firmly believes that the way a shifter treats a species weaker than himself is very telling of their home life.

Mycroft doesn't even make it to the bar before the scent of his mate hits his senses, distracting him. Unable to help himself, he leaves the reconnaissance to Dakota in order to track down the other half of his soul. To his surprise, Mycroft realizes his special someone is a vampire—Boyd Johnson. While the timing is terrible, Mycroft trusts in Fate's plan. Can he figure out how to complete his mission while giving Boyd the time and attention they need to forge their bond?

With Cheetah Speed
Copyright © 2022 Charlie Richards
ISBN: 978-1-4874-3602-5
Cover art by Angela Waters

Published by eXtasy Books Inc

Look for us online at:
www.eXtasybooks.com

WITH CHEETAH SPEED
A LOVING NIP BOOK TWENTY-EIGHT

BY

CHARLIE RICHARDS

DEDICATION

When life comes at you fast, it's not always a bad thing.

CHAPTER ONE

Scrolling through the reports on his tablet's screen, Mycroft Portent mentally cataloged who his available enforcers and investigators were and who would be best suited for each task. As the head council enforcer, he oversaw the duties of every man and woman who worked for the Shifter Council, from the enforcers to those who worked in the kitchens and those who tended the lawns. The only ones who didn't report to Mycroft were the councilmen themselves, although he normally knew each of their schedules, simply for security reasons.

Mycroft had fought hard for his position, and he wouldn't trade it for anything, regardless of how it seemed to have taken over his life.

It's worth it. It's worth it to help safeguard our species.

Having a front-row seat to the revelation that there had been corruption within the ranks of the Shifter Council had caused Mycroft's gut to twist with revulsion. He believed the position of Shifter Councilman—or woman, although they hadn't had one for several decades—was a sacred position of trust. While carrying the title of councilman came with certain privileges, they should have been focused on using those perks for the betterment of their kind rather than lining their own pockets and attempting to gain more power for themselves.

It had been a disgusting display of the avarice that could corrupt any species.

Mycroft pushed the memories away and returned his attention to his tablet. To his relief, he realized he had three investigators available, so he quickly assigned them each a duty, forwarding the corresponding report to each of them. When Mycroft reviewed who was available within the shifter enforcers, he grimaced.

While Mycroft was happy for the enforcers who'd recently been blessed with their fated mates, it created problems for him. Several were on vacation, cementing their bonds. That left him shorthanded.

There were four files, but he had only five enforcers free. Due to the fact that they would be traveling into possibly hostile territory, he liked to send them in pairs. They needed their backs watched because they were normally going there to roust some or all of the inner circle.

Rubbing his palm over his face, Mycroft realized he would need to reassign some people. He glanced through the files of who was assigned to which councilman as protection within the halls of Shifter Headquarters, counting heads. Humming, he chose two and made the necessary calls, letting not only the enforcers know of their change in duties, but the affected councilmen. That way, if the councilman chose to, they could bring an extra guard from their private estate to supplement.

As Mycroft began searching for a final shifter to reallocate, a thought struck him.

I could go. I can do this work on the road.

Mycroft hesitated a moment, indecision filling him. Then it occurred to him that this would be like a vacation for him. He could get out of the office, get his bike out, and enjoy the open road a little before arriving in the area around Amarillo, Texas where the cougar pride in question was located.

My bike. Hmmm . . .

The cheetah Mycroft shared his psyche with rumbled in his mind. His animal seemed to like the idea. He could fly down the streets on the back of his 2021 *CBR1000RR-R Fireblade SP.*

He'd had the street-legal racing motorcycle custom painted with a cheetah coloring design, and he'd just gotten it back two weeks prior, but he hadn't had a chance to take it out, yet.

It'll almost be like running in animal form.

Unable to stop himself from grinning, Mycroft made a quick switch on his assignments. He ordered Enforcer Lyra to go with Enforcer Rigel, freeing Enforcer Dakota. Then he picked up his phone to call Dakota himself in regards to the changes.

"Hi, Enforcer Mycroft," Dakota greeted, answering on the second ring. "I just saw the alert about the change. Is everything okay?"

"Yes, Dakota," Mycroft replied, dropping titles, knowing the other shifter would do the same. "I sent you a follow-up file. I need you to go to Texas instead."

"Sure." Dakota chuckled, adding, "Nice open roads in Texas."

Mycroft smirked. "I thought you'd like that."

"Absolutely." After a second of hesitation, Dakota added, "It doesn't say who I'm traveling with. What if they don't have a bike?"

"He has a bike," Mycroft assured, grinning. "You're traveling with me."

"You?" Dakota's shock came through the line, loud and clear.

Mycroft chuckled. "Yes, me. Don't sound so shocked," he teased.

"I, well, huh." Dakota's happy-go-lucky chuckle came through the line. "Just can't remember the last time you went out on an assignment."

"I was thinking the same thing," Mycroft admitted. "Which is why, since we're so short-staffed with so many finding their fated mates, I thought I'd pitch in." Scoffing softly, Mycroft added, "Besides, I can keep up on files from over the road, and this'll be like a vacation for me."

Dakota laughed again. "Sure thing, boss-man. Where and when do we meet?"

"I'll give you a little time to review the file," Mycroft told him as he rose to his feet. "I'll meet you at the gas station on Third and Sommers at five-thirty. It's close to the freeway in the direction we need out of town."

"Got it," Dakota replied. He sounded a little confused as he added, "Three hours is more than enough. Why so long?"

Mycroft grinned broadly. "Thought a little night racing would be fun."

A soft growl entered Dakota's voice as he repeated, "Night racing?"

A low chuckle escaped Mycroft. He knew he'd piqued Dakota's competitive side. The Komodo dragon shifter had two older brothers, and he knew all of them enjoyed a good competition.

"That's right," Mycroft replied, grinning. "Night racing."

"You're on, Mycroft." Dakota's pleasure could be heard in his voice as he added, "But don't think I'll let you win just because you're my boss."

Mycroft locked his office as he replied, "I won't need you to *let me*." Not giving the other shifter a chance to quip back, he added, "See you there, Dakota."

Then Mycroft disconnected the line. He had a few things to take care of before he could head out. With that in mind, he hurried toward the elevator with the intent of tracking down Councilman Regales Colearian. Mycroft needed to speak to at least one councilman, technically to ask permission, but he knew it wouldn't be an issue.

Upon receiving Regales's blessing, Mycroft headed home. He parked his quad-cab pick-up in the detached two-car garage of his Tudor-style home. Mycroft had bought it as a fixer-upper nearly a decade before and had removed a wall between two bedrooms facing the back, installed a bank of massive windows, and created a sunroom for his cheetah.

Unknown to anyone, Mycroft loved to unwind by basking.

Right then, however, Mycroft was looking forward to doing something else he loved — riding his motorcycle at excessive speeds. He couldn't say it was a cheetah thing because Dakota wasn't a cheetah. Mycroft knew the Komodo dragon shifter enjoyed the activity just as much, and he couldn't wait to pit his skills against the other man.

Mycroft made quick work of a shower. After drying off, he padded nude around his space, packing a couple changes of clothes into a duffle bag. His tablet went into a padded case, which he placed between the folds of his jeans. Mycroft tossed his bathroom kit on top and zipped the bag closed.

After dressing in a pair of comfortable jeans and a dark green polo shirt, Mycroft headed to his kitchen. He grabbed a plastic container full of leftover bacon-wrapped, cheese-filled jalapenos and popped the lid. Licking his lips, Mycroft anticipated enjoying the leftover wedding reception food.

As Mycroft placed eight of the tasty morsels onto a plate and shoved them in the microwave to heat for a minute, he smiled as he thought about Dane and Danny's wedding. The pair had been married a week prior, and he'd had the privilege of witnessing the unusual event. Most shifters didn't bother marrying their human mate, since claiming their mate — bonding them and twining their life forces in the paranormal way — was far more permanent than any ceremony a human could devise.

Still, having seen the way Danny lit up with happiness as they'd exchanged their vows, Mycroft had understood why Dane had done it.

We'll do just about anything to please our mate.

The microwave dinged, drawing Mycroft out of his pleasant memories. Before Councilman Regales Colearian had found his mate while visiting a wolf shifter pack led by a gay alpha, which had started a rush of others in the area finding fated mates, Mycroft hadn't really thought much about finding his own mate. With them popping up all over the place, though, he couldn't help but wonder.

What will my mate be like?

Mycroft pulled his food out and carried it to the table. He knew he couldn't even imagine. After all, who would have guessed that Fate would give their badass head interrogator—Delanrue Drudeson—a tiny guinea pig shifter as a mate—Miggs.

Oddly enough, they complemented each other perfectly. Miggs received a huge, powerful champion to keep him safe and secure in Delanrue. Delanrue was granted a sweet, loving man to remind him of his conscience and how to live life.

Mycroft could only guess at what Fate thought he needed.

An hour later, Mycroft geared up. He pulled his leathers on over his jeans. His plated leather jacket offered an extra layer of protection for his torso. He slipped his full helmet on top of his head.

Smiling behind his face shield, Mycroft swung his leg over his high-end motorcycle. The whine of the engine roaring to life caused a thrill to run through him. He rolled his motorcycle out of his garage, then pushed a button to close the door.

Turning his wheel to the right, Mycroft hit the throttle and started down his driveway. He barely resisted gunning the engine when he reached the road. His excitement mounted as he made his way through the streets to the gas station where he'd told Dakota to meet him.

Will be out of town soon enough. Then I'll open her up.

Mycroft parked at a gas pump and swung off. As he was in the middle of filling his motorcycle, he spotted Dakota turning into the station on his metallic purple *Kawasaki Ninja* motorcycle. The enforcer must have noticed him, too, for he headed directly toward him, stopping close.

Straightening, Dakota flipped up his visor and grinned at him. "Damn, Mycroft. When did you have her painted?"

"She was in the shop for a month," Mycroft admitted, easing the nozzle from his tank's hole. "Just got her back about two weeks ago." Holding up the handle, Mycroft offered, "Top off?"

"Don't mind if I do." Dakota took the offered pump handle in one hand before opening the gas tank with the other. "Well, it's a sweet look." After a furtive glance around, Dakota lowered his voice and asked, "They your cat's spots?"

Mycroft grinned as he screwed his gas cap back on. "Good eye, Dakota. That they are."

While Dakota topped off his tank, he murmured, "Observant. That's me."

After letting out a snort, Mycroft took the nozzle back and hung it back on the pump. He took the receipt and shoved it into his pocket. Mycroft swung onto his bike and brought it roaring back to life.

"I've sent you the route we're taking for our best chance of staying off the cop's radar." Pinning Dakota with a competitive stare, Mycroft stated, "First one to the hotel gets to choose their room in the two-bedroom suite I booked."

Barking a laugh, Dakota responded, "You're on."

Forty-five minutes later, when they were well out of town, Mycroft glanced Dakota's way. He found the other man peering right back at him. When he spotted the way the Komodo dragon shifter twisted his throttle, Mycroft grinned and did the same.

As one, they shot forward, their engines revving as they barreled down the road, ignoring every traffic law known to man.

"Told you I'd win," Mycroft cajoled as he removed his helmet from his head. He rested it on a handlebar as he added, "Now stop your bitching. I'll buy you a beer."

As Dakota heaved a deep sigh, he rolled his eyes. A second later, he grinned at Mycroft. "A beer would be good." Then he sobered as he peered at what appeared to be a run-down honky-tonk bar, which was situated on the outskirts of a small town near Amarillo. "You sure this is where Beta Bradley and Enforcer Parakesh like to hang out?"

Mycroft nodded. "According to our tech guys, it is." He'd had an investigator track the money trail of every member of the inner circle, allowing them to know where each cougar shifter in the inner circle spent their time and money while off pride lands. Resting his hands on his hips, he eyed the place. "There'll probably be a few other members of the pride in there, too, so we'll need to watch our step."

Dakota grinned broadly as he ran his fingers through his short blond hair. "Will do, sir."

"Mycroft," he corrected softly as he headed toward the bar's entrance. "We're drinking buddies. Remember?"

"Yep." To Mycroft's surprise, Dakota slung his arm around his shoulders and bumped into him a little. Raising his voice, probably so the ladies entering the door heard him, he added, "Let's get our groove on, man. I feel the need to dance."

Going with it, Mycroft grinned as he replied, "You know it." When Dakota opened the door for him, he entered. A quick scan of the room showed him the lay of the land. As Mycroft noticed the cougar shifters in the left corner occupying the pool tables, he started toward the bar. "Let me get you that drink, Dakota."

Even as Mycroft registered Dakota's nod in the peripheral of his vision, a scent tickled his senses, drawing not just his attention, but that of his cat's. His cheetah perked up in his mind, and Mycroft couldn't help taking a deeper breath. The scent of pine mixed with . . . cattle . . . tugged at his attention. It caused his blood to heat as arousal surged through him.

"Oh, fuck," Mycroft muttered, missing a step as he realized what it meant.

"What's wrong?" Dakota paused, his hand on his upper arm. He was scanning the room as he whispered, "What do you sense?"

"My mate is in the room," Mycroft blurted out.

Dakota snapped his attention to Mycroft as his blond brows shot up his forehead. A grin curved his lips. Still, the other shifter remained professional, his voice coming out level.

"Well, fuck, man." Dakota squeezed Mycroft's arm as he offered, "Congrats."

"Thanks," Mycroft instantly responded. "Just bad timing."

Tightening his grip, Dakota forced Mycroft to a stop, and he met the other shifter's gaze.

With an encouraging smile, Dakota told him, "It's never bad timing to find your mate."

Mycroft scoffed softly as he nodded once. "You're right."

"Course I am." Then Dakota winked and released him. "I'll get my own beer and keep an eye on our friends. You go find your mate."

After a nod and a murmured thanks, Mycroft did as his cheetah insisted. He began a slow prowl of the room, searching for that special person who gave off the euphoric scent.

Chapter Two

For some reason, Boyd Johnson suddenly felt his interest in his dance partner wane. The erection he'd been sporting eased, and his thirst for her blood dried up. While Boyd didn't understand why he was suddenly no longer attracted to the female human, he never second-guessed his vampiric nature.

If his sixth sense told him to back away from someone, Boyd did it.

Now I just have to figure out how to do that.

Boyd couldn't very well trance the woman in the middle of a crowded bar, sending her on her way. His red irises would be a little hard to explain. Also, considering how his dance partner clung to him like a barnacle as they two-stepped around the dance floor, Boyd didn't think a brush-off would do anything but cause a scene.

As a vampire, Boyd liked to keep a low profile. Scenes were not his thing. He enjoyed discreetly picking up a donor — male or female didn't really matter to him as long as the scent was right. He would slip out a back door into the alley or go into a bathroom stall and enjoy the flavor of his partner's blood. Most times, Boyd had no problem screwing said partner while blurring their memory of the bite.

Right then, however, the idea of banging the slender brunette held no appeal.

Boyd glanced to the left as he rounded the dance floor. To his relief, he saw that Murdoch was back at their table with his beloved, Malakai. With a tilt of his chin, Boyd snagged Murdoch's attention. Ever so discreetly, he made the abort signal behind his dance partner's back.

Murdoch's pale-blue eyes widened just a smidge before he jerked a nod.

As Boyd swept past the table, he saw the way his fellow vampire leaned over and whispered something into his beloved's ear. Malakai's brows furrowed a little, but he didn't respond. If Boyd had to guess, they were probably speaking telepathically. Once a vampire bonded with their beloved, regardless of species, their minds would be linked, allowing them to share thoughts and feelings.

Boyd could hardly wait. Every time he watched a new vehicle arrive at their coven's dude ranch, he wondered if his beloved was inside it. Every time he left the ranch to hang out with friends and find a donor, Boyd hoped he would meet that special someone.

Sadly, so far, it hadn't happened.

While Boyd knew he was young at one-hundred-twelve years old, that didn't mean he wasn't affected by disappointment.

And now, this chick isn't doing it for me.

"Excuse me. May I cut in?"

To Boyd's surprise, the soft tenor in his ear caused heat to thrum through his veins. He half spun in surprise. Peering over his shoulder, he swept his gaze over a muscular male whose thick red hair appeared finger-combed into submission. Boyd's mouth began to water as he admired his worn, comfortable-looking jeans and frame-hugging polo shirt.

The guy could have just rolled out of the sack and never looked better.

Hearing the woman on his arm titter and murmur, "Not at all," before she released Boyd and reached toward the stranger grated on Boyd's last nerve. His fingers twitched, but not with the desire to hold onto his dance partner. Instead, he wanted to yank her away from the man and grab ahold of the guy himself.

Then . . . even more shock surged through Boyd as he watched the man brush aside the woman's reaching hands. "I'm sorry, ma'am," the stranger murmured. "You misunderstand." He offered her a slight smile before turning to Boyd and holding out his right hand. "I mean, I would like to dance with *you*." Then, his green-eyed gaze steady, he stared at Boyd.

Shocked, Boyd hesitated. "R-Really?"

The redheaded stranger's full lips curved into a slight smile. "Really."

"Uh, okay."

Boyd knew that the bar didn't have a problem with two dudes dancing together. He'd seen others do it. He'd just never had anyone ask him before. Normally, Boyd was the aggressor.

Even before Boyd managed to slide his palm into the guy's hand, the woman snapped, "Are you serious?"

The redhead barely spared the brunette a glance as he replied, "I am." With a smile, he wiggled his fingers. "Don't leave me hanging, mate."

While Boyd finally finished the move to clasp the man's hand, the stranger's scent reached his nostrils—fresh wind and something definitely feline. It caused his mouth to water, and his fangs began to ache. The glide of his hand against the other man's caused the hairs on his arm to stand on end, and two things hit him at once. The man who'd asked him to dance was a shifter, and he was most likely the other half of his soul.

"Beloved," Boyd whispered, unable to keep the thought to himself.

"You're gay?" the brunette snarled, drawing his attention. "Why the hell did you dance with me then?" Curling her lip, she glared at him. "What? You were hoping I'd be your beard or something?"

Boyd shook his head. "I'm bi, actually, and I was attracted to you." *Was* being the operative word. Before she could come up with something else, he peered at the shifter, meeting his intense green-eyed gaze. "And you were about to accept a dance with him, so you recognize his appeal." With a shrug, Boyd finished, "Why would I be different?"

Upon seeing the sides of the shifter's lips curve into a small smile, Boyd felt as if his heart skipped a beat.

"Thank you," the man murmured.

To Boyd's relief, the woman just huffed a sigh before pivoting and stalking from the dance floor.

When the shifter moved his arms into position — one hand on Boyd's hip while clasping his hand with the other, taking the role of the dance lead — he was too shocked at the unexpected turn of events to counter it. Besides, he recognized the dominance in the slightly shorter male. Boyd relaxed into the role of follower, accepting the shifter's guidance, staring into the other man's eyes in wonder.

They hadn't even made it a full loop around the dance floor when Boyd blurted out, "Who are you?"

With a low chuckle, the redhead replied, "Right. The pleasantries." He smirked as he admitted, "I'm afraid running into my mate in this backwater honky-tonk has scattered my focus. I'm Mycroft Portent. And you are?"

"Boyd Johnson," he immediately replied. Lowering his voice, he added, "I scent your cat. Are you part of the cougar pride?"

Has my beloved been right under my nose for decades?

Their vampire coven didn't have much contact with the cougar pride, normally only running across a member in the occasional bar. When Boyd and his friends had arrived at the dive bar, they'd spotted Beta Bradley and a few others, and had considered leaving. Boyd's gut had urged him to stay, and never would he be more grateful that he'd followed his gut.

Mycroft shook his head. "No, I work for the Shifter Council," he replied, his words so soft that Boyd barely made them out with his sensitive vampire hearing. "I'm supposed to be looking into them, but you have . . . distracted me."

With a grimace, Mycroft glanced toward the bar.

Following his gaze, Boyd spotted a large man with ear-length blond hair. He held a beer in one hand and chatted with the woman beside him. Still, Boyd could see that the guy was keeping an eye on everything that was happening around him—especially them dancing as well as the cougar shifters at the pool table.

"I can't say that I'm sorry," Boyd insisted, hoping to re-draw the shifter's attention. "Finding your other half is a blessing."

Mycroft snapped his focus back to Boyd, his eyes widening just a smidge. "Of course it is." He squeezed Boyd's hip. "Please, don't think I meant otherwise."

Boyd nodded once. "Okay." As much as he enjoyed dancing with the man, he knew they really needed privacy. He dipped his head and murmured, "We need a private corner so I can taste you, and we can have a serious conversation."

"Agreed." Mycroft offered a small smile, adding, "Not that I don't really enjoy dancing with you." After squeezing his hand, Mycroft adjusted their palms, twining their fingers together. "I need to talk to Dakota before we leave."

While Boyd hadn't intended for them to just up and leave, he didn't counter the shifter. He was experiencing a burning desire to taste Mycroft, to confirm that he was indeed his beloved. Boyd figured he could trust the cat shifter's claim, but a vampire could only be one hundred percent sure by tasting their beloved's blood—and Boyd's mouth watered with his need.

Just as they reached the big man's side—Dakota, Boyd figured—Murdoch and Malakai appeared, joining them.

"Hey, Boyd," Murdoch greeted, a questioning smile curving his lips after he sniffed discreetly. "Everything okay?"

"Yeah," Boyd assured, offering his friend a reassuring smile. "Murdoch, this is Mycroft and his friend, Dakota."

At his words, Dakota excused himself from the woman, who appeared disappointed but still turned away. The blond grinned broadly and held out his hand. "So this is him, huh, Mycroft?"

"He is," Mycroft confirmed, releasing his hand so they could shake only to wrap his arm around his waist. "I'm not certain how much use I'll be to you for the rest of the evening."

Dakota released Boyd, then leaned against the bar. "Well, we hadn't planned on engaging tonight anyway. I'll be fine."

Boyd could guess at the meaning of the man's words—some kind of shifter that he couldn't get a read on—but he offered, "If it has to do with the report submitted on our friends at the pool table, buy my buddies a drink." Boyd quickly introduced Murdoch and Malakai. "They have first-hand knowledge and can answer questions."

After downing the rest of his beer, Dakota set the empty bottle on the bar. "Sounds good." He grinned broadly at the pair as he signaled for the bartender. "What can I get you guys?" Once they'd made their requests, Dakota winked at Mycroft and stated, "You have a good night, boss-man."

Mycroft's smile appeared a little feral as he focused on Boyd. "I'm sure I will."

A fissure of heat danced up Boyd's spine, causing his gut to clench. His dick thickened to full mast, pressing painfully against the fly of his jeans. Even his gut clenched, and for the first time in nearly a century, Boyd felt butterflies dance in his stomach.

Before Boyd could think up a response, Murdoch cut in. "Congrats, Boyd." With a wink, he added, "Don't forget to call Jaymes."

"I won't," Boyd replied.

"Come on, my mate," Mycroft rumbled. "Time to go some-where . . . quieter."

Boyd was plenty on board with that, and he enjoyed My-croft's possessive hand on his lower back as he guided him out the door.

"Your friends will have Dakota's back if something hap-pens?" Mycroft questioned once they'd cleared the door, ob-viously concerned for his co-worker. Moving away from the building and prying ears, he added, "Murdoch is a vampire, but Malakai is something else. Care to share?"

"Angel," Boyd replied. "And yeah. They'll be good."

Mycroft hummed in acknowledgment. "Thank you."

"For?" Boyd wasn't following. He was way too focused on the heat of the palm at his back and wondering what it would feel like pressed against his bare flesh.

"Giving Dakota back-up, even though he probably won't need it." Mycroft paused, sliding his arms around Boyd's waist to draw him to a stop as well. "When I walked into that bar and knew my mate was somewhere inside, I was wor-ried." Peering up their inch difference in height, Mycroft ad-mitted, "As much as I appreciate finding you, leaving him alone to carry out our surveillance made me extremely un-comfortable."

Wrapping his arms around Mycroft, Boyd returned the embrace, and he enjoyed a shiver of delight upon holding the other man. "He called you boss-man," he mused as he peered into the shifter's vibrant eyes.

Mycroft nodded once. "Yes, but I'll explain that later." Tip-ping his head to the side a little, he rumbled huskily, "I think there's something else you'd like to confirm first."

Groaning, Boyd zeroed in on Mycroft's pulse point. He licked his lips before swallowing hard. A quick glance around told him that they were alone in the dark parking lot.

Unable to resist Mycroft's offer, Boyd lowered his head, whispering, "Just a scratch to confirm."

Then Boyd licked over the shifter's pulse point, tasting light sweat and the other man's delicious flesh. He did it a second time, then a third, before scraping one fang over the saliva-coated skin. When the bead of blood that oozed up hit Boyd's tongue, he groaned. The exquisite flavor exploded over his taste buds, rocking his senses, and sending all his good intentions floating away on the wind.

My beloved!

Boyd sank his fangs deep into Mycroft's flesh and sucked, drinking deeply of the man Fate had deemed his.

CHAPTER THREE

Mycroft felt the first nick of Boyd's fang, causing a tingling pleasure to heat his chest. While he'd heard that a vampire's bite was enjoyable, in the over two-hundred-fifty years of his life, he'd never experienced it. He smiled upon feeling the sensation, wondering what a full bite would feel like.

A second later, Mycroft found out.

Having obviously lost control of his nature upon tasting the blood of his beloved, Boyd sank his fangs deep inside his flesh.

After just the briefest flash of pain, euphoria rushed through Mycroft's veins. He groaned, his eyelids sliding closed as ecstasy shot through him. Each sucking pull on his neck felt as if it transferred straight to his rock-hard cock. In seconds, Mycroft's balls pulled tight, and he found himself doing something he couldn't recall doing . . . ever.

Mycroft's orgasm roared through his system, and he unloaded in his jeans. His body bucked, shuddering. He felt certain he would have melted into the gravel beneath his booted feet if it weren't for Boyd's strong arms holding him tight against his wiry frame.

Spots were dancing across Mycroft's vision when Boyd eased his teeth from him. He felt his mate lick across the wound, sealing the marks. At first, Mycroft had trouble making out the man's words, but finally, they registered.

"Sorry. I'm so sorry," Boyd whispered against his neck, still not having raised his head. He clutched Mycroft to his chest, holding him tightly, as if in fear that he would flee. "Please forgive me, beloved. I'm sorry."

"Hush, Boyd," Mycroft murmured, managing to find his tongue. Gathering a bit of coordination, he rubbed his palms up and down his vampire's spine, trying to soothe him. "There is nothing to forgive." Mycroft turned his head and pressed a kiss to Boyd's neck. When he still didn't lift his head to meet his gaze, Mycroft reminded, "I'm a shifter. It gives me great pleasure to meet your needs." Then a breeze kicked up, blowing across his wet crotch, and Mycroft chuckled roughly. "Literally." With a squeeze to the back of Boyd's neck, he added, "But I would very much like to get out of these soaked jeans. Will you come with me to my hotel suite?"

Boyd finally lifted his head and met Mycroft's gaze. "Even after my lapse, you still wish to spend the evening with me?"

Mycroft sighed deeply, cradling Boyd's jaw. Seeing the uncertainty in the slightly taller man's blue eyes, he tried to figure out from where it stemmed. "Boyd, you are my mate. I knew you were a vampire when I offered you my neck." He smirked as he added, "And you can bite me any damn time you want." Wincing, Mycroft had to add, "Well, maybe not in front of kids."

To Mycroft's relief, the uncertainty eased from Boyd's eyes. "Sorry," the vampire repeated once more. Fortunately, he followed it up with an explanation. "Guess I've watched so many of my friends get bonded with a human that I forgot how straight-forward it can be with another paranormal."

Pleased, Mycroft nodded. "Exactly." After another squeeze to Boyd's neck, he released him. "Where's your ride? Will you follow me to my hotel?"

"I came with Murdoch and Malakai," Boyd revealed with a shrug. "Can I hitch a ride with you?"

"Of course." Mycroft indicated the motorcycle he stood beside. "As long as you don't mind riding bitch."

Boyd turned his attention to Mycroft's high-end racing motorcycle and whistled appreciatively. "Damn." After a second of obvious hesitation, he reached out and ran his fingertips along one cheetah-colored fender. "Is this your animal? A cheetah?"

Mycroft nodded. "It is."

"Running together is going to be so much fun," Boyd murmured.

Smirking, Mycroft teased, "Think you can keep up with me?" He knew vampires could run incredibly fast, but he hadn't seen one in action in quite some time.

Boyd chuckled as he grinned at him. "I'll give it my best damn shot." Then he shifted his weight from foot to foot and pulled at the fly of his jeans. "But right now, a shower wouldn't be remiss."

That was when it hit Mycroft. Boyd had gotten off on drinking his blood. Mycroft hummed in satisfaction, inordinately pleased by that knowledge.

"The hotel and a shower," Mycroft agreed. Picking up his helmet, he held it out to Boyd. He spotted the male's denial a mile away and urged, "Indulge me, my mate. Please."

Boyd sighed but took the helmet.

As his vampire buckled it on, Mycroft swung a leg over his bike. He had to look for a few seconds to locate the bitch seat foot-pegs so he could bend them into position. Mycroft couldn't remember the last time he'd carried a passenger on his motorcycle.

Huh. Don't think I ever have.

Mycroft's *Fireblade* wasn't truly made for two people, but they would make it work.

Actually, I like the idea of having my vampire flushed over my back, holding onto me tightly.

With a smile, Mycroft brought his motorcycle roaring to life. He held out his hand, palm up, offering assistance. To his pleasure, Boyd accepted the offer, allowing him to help him onto the tiny bitch seat behind him.

Once Boyd had wrapped his arms tightly around him, Mycroft started them moving. He kept his speed relatively slow, more to get used to having a passenger than because he worried about scaring or harming Boyd. While Mycroft never wanted to intentionally hurt his mate, he knew vampires were tough to take out and bounced back from injuries swiftly.

Damn. Fate is good to me. She's given me a mate who can stand by my side against other paranormals.

Mycroft had been a little worried he would end up with a human. While he had nothing against the species, they were weaker, simply by design. He couldn't imagine how difficult it was for his enforcers to always have the concern of their mate niggling in the backs of their minds.

Due to the whine of the powerful engine, Mycroft didn't try to make small talk on the drive to the hotel. Boyd must have been of the same mind, for he remained quiet, too. Mycroft parked near a side entrance and shut off the bike.

Once Boyd stood on his own two feet and pulled off the helmet, he grinned at him. "Were you driving like that for my benefit?" he teased. "If so, I hope we can find time to go a hell of a lot faster."

Chuckling softly, Mycroft dismounted. He couldn't resist pulling Boyd into his arms. "Are you a speed demon?" he teased.

"A little," Boyd admitted, returning his embrace. "So?"

"Mostly for my benefit, actually," Mycroft admitted. Seeing Boyd's confusion, he told him, "I've never taken a passenger on this bike. I was learning the balance of it."

Boyd grinned widely. "Well, I'm honored. Thanks."

Mycroft eyed Boyd's full lips, and the desire to kiss the man surged through him. He'd just started to tip his head while lifting his hand to his vampire's nape when the sound of laughter drew his attention. Peering left, Mycroft spotted a couple with two small children entering the front of the hotel. The toddler in the woman's arms was bouncing and laughing at something one of them must have said or did.

Seeing that reminded Mycroft of where they stood.

With a sigh, Mycroft eased away from Boyd. Fortunately, his vampire appeared to have followed his focus and understood.

"As soon as we get in that shower, your mouth is mine," Boyd vowed.

Mycroft growled softly as he grinned at Boyd. "Looking forward to it."

Turning, Mycroft headed to the side entrance. He used his door key to unlock it, and he led the way inside. "You okay with stairs?" Mycroft asked, gripping the handle to the stairwell. "Fifth floor."

Boyd nodded. "That's fine."

With a nod, Mycroft entered the stairwell. He took them two at a time, pleased to see Boyd easily keeping pace. They reached the fifth floor in record time, and Mycroft led the way to his room. After inserting the key and waiting for the light to turn green, he opened the door and headed inside.

As if perfectly in sync with Mycroft, Boyd didn't bother saying a word. Instead, his vampire reached for the hem of his shirt, just as Mycroft did. As they moved through the central room, they tossed their shirts on a chair. Then they both paused to pull off their boots—Mycroft's motorcycle boots and Boyd his cowboy boots. Their socks quickly followed.

Leading the way through his bedroom, Mycroft unzipped his fly. He winced as he peeled the flaps away from his half-hard prick. The cum had begun to dry, causing his pubic hairs to tug at his skin. By the time Mycroft reached his room's bathroom ensuite, he could shove his jeans down and off, which he did.

Hearing Boyd's appreciative whistle, Mycroft turned to

find an equally nude vampire standing in the doorway. He saw the feral desire in his red-irised eyes. The fact that Boyd's eyes had hazed gave away his need just as clearly as the hard cock jutting from his groin.

Mycroft backed up slowly, admiring Fate's gift.

Boyd stood an inch taller than Mycroft's own six-foot-one. His body was a roadmap of tanned, toned muscle, obviously carved from hard work. There was a thin scar marring his left pectoral, telling Mycroft that Boyd had seen his fair share of danger and had come out the victor.

Lifting his hand, Mycroft beckoned Boyd toward him. "You are stunning, my mate," he rumbled even as he reached back with his other hand and opened the shower stall door. Having chosen a nice, two-bedroom suite for himself and Dakota, there would be plenty of space for both of them. "Let's get to that shower, so we can move on to other pleasurable endeavors."

The corner of Boyd's mouth kicked up into a roguish smile. "Who says the shower itself won't be pleasurable?" As he started forward, his attention flicked to Mycroft's groin, where his cock had quickly filled to full mast upon enjoying the view of his naked vampire. "I can think of nothing more enjoyable than completing our bond. Got lube in there?"

Mycroft felt his shaft throb, twitching at his groin. "Lube," he muttered. Shaking his head, he admitted, "I'm here on assignment. I didn't even think to bring any with me."

Boyd held up the jeans he still held in his hand. "Well." Clearing his throat, his cheeks taking on a pinkish hue, he pulled a single-use packet from his front pocket. "It's not waterproof, but we can make it work, right?"

A low snarl erupted from Mycroft as a surge of jealousy ripped through him upon seeing the proof that his mate had intended to pick up someone at the bar that night. He knew it was irrational, but he couldn't seem to stop himself. Lunging forward, Mycroft grabbed Boyd by his upper arms and yanked him close, getting in his face.

"You're mine!"

A second later, Mycroft sank his extended canines deep into his vampire's flesh where his neck met his shoulder, claiming what was his.

CHAPTER FOUR

Boyd roared, his back arching — not from pain, but from pleasure.

One second, Mycroft was turning on the shower. The next instant, he was across the bathroom and sinking his teeth into Boyd's neck. While there had been an instant of pain, it had morphed so quickly into blissful zings, which had gone straight to Boyd's balls, that it was as if he hadn't felt it at all.

His balls pulled tight, and his cock throbbed. Fire coursed through his veins. The second sucking sensation to his neck caused an orgasm of epic proportions to surge through him.

Boyd gripped Mycroft's upper arms in a mirror hold — not to push him away, but simply to steady himself. His body shook with the intensity of his release, shudders racking him. Each pulse of his spurting cock created new shock waves within him, and spots danced across his vision.

Vaguely, Boyd felt something warm splash across his abdominals, telling him that Mycroft was coming, too.

When Mycroft eased his teeth from his flesh and lapped over the wound, Boyd sighed deeply as fresh tingles danced across his skin.

"Mycroft," Boyd whispered roughly, his fingers tightening and easing as he did his best not to sway.

Mycroft heaved a sigh before resting his temple against Boyd's. "Now it's my turn to apologize," he muttered. "I saw you pull out that package and remembered you dancing with that woman and . . . gods, I just saw red."

Boyd cradled Mycroft's jaw and urged him to ease away.

Meeting his beloved's gaze, he smiled. "Neither one of us was a virgin when we met tonight," he murmured. "We both know that." Giving in to his need, Boyd pressed a chaste kiss to Mycroft's lips. "But if it makes you feel any better, I'd already been trying to figure out a way to extricate myself from the woman I was dancing with."

The corners of Mycroft's lips curved up a smidge. "Oddly enough, it does." He nuzzled into Boyd's hold in a move very reminiscent of his cat looking for attention. "But why?"

Sliding his arm lower, Boyd wrapped it around Mycroft's waist. He used the hold to turn his beloved, pleased when the shifter moved willingly. While Boyd wasn't a dominant male by any means, he wanted the opportunity to care for his soul mate, too.

"Well," Boyd began, urging Mycroft into the shower. "As we danced, something in me lost interest. In fact, my nature started urging me to distance myself from her." Closing the door behind them, Boyd eased them both under the hot spray. "My guess is that some sixth sense told me that you'd entered the bar, that I needed to wait for another."

Boyd placed the single-use lube packet on the shelf in favor of picking up the complimentary shampoo bottle. After pouring some onto his palm, he lifted his hands to his shifter's head. He threaded his fingers into Mycroft's hair, scrubbing his scalp lightly.

Mycroft sighed deeply and bowed his head for Boyd's ministrations. "That feels so good," he murmured on a groan.

"While we wash, since we've taken the edge off"—Boyd paused and chuckled—"we can take a few moments to share a little about ourselves without the driving need to bond clouding our minds with lust."

To Boyd's pleasure, Mycroft's lips twitched, and he nodded infinitesimally. "Okay. I'm a cheetah shifter, as you know." He hesitated an instant before peering at Mycroft from beneath his lashes, holding his gaze as he revealed, "I'm two-hundred-sixty-nine years old, and for the last hundred years or so, I've worked for the Shifter Council. I was hired on as an enforcer, but I worked damn hard, rose up the ranks, and now I hold the position of Head Enforcer for the Shifter Council."

Boyd paused for a few seconds before urging Mycroft to tilt his head back so he could rinse the soap from his hair. As he did that, he gave that news the consideration it was due. He recalled Dakota calling him boss-man, and now that made perfect sense. His beloved was a very important man in the shifter world.

"That's impressive," Boyd murmured, moving on to grab the soap. "I imagine it took a hell of a lot of discipline and training to achieve that status."

Mycroft nodded. "It did." Then he shrugged dismissively. "But at the end of the day, I love to go home, turn into my cheetah, and lounge in my sunroom, so I figure I'm not that different than any other shifter."

Boyd nodded, guessing at what Mycroft was telling him. "Your job is just what you do, not who you are."

"Right." Mycroft sounded pleased that Boyd had figured it out. "You knew of the incident with the cougar shifter pride, so am I right to assume you're part of the coven led by Master Jaymes Martinez located north of Amarillo?"

"I am," Boyd confirmed. "I work with the horses and take guests on trail rides." Scoffing softly, he couldn't help but add, "Not nearly as prestigious as your job, but I enjoy it."

Mycroft sucked in a sharp breath when Boyd rubbed his thumb around one nipple, and he couldn't help but grin.

"Well," Mycroft began huskily. "I'm sure your master considers you important."

Boyd hummed as he rubbed his palms down Mycroft's

lean torso. Admiring his beloved's trim waist and lightly de-fined abdominals, he nodded absently. His master was a fan-tastic leader, giving as much opportunity as possible to all his people.

Reaching Mycroft's groin, Boyd found his lover's dick once again hard, jutting enticingly from his groin. His mouth wa-tered as he gripped his shifter's long slender prick in one hand. Boyd appreciated a long cock, looking forward to feel-ing his length burrowing deep inside his ass. With his other hand, Boyd gently cupped Mycroft's balls, rolling and squeezing them, getting a feel for his shifter's sensitivity level.

Mycroft groaned softly, bucking into his hold. Resting his hands on Boyd's shoulders, he began rocking his hips.

"Gods, the tales of excessive randiness when meeting your fated mate are true," Mycroft muttered gruffly. "Hard again already. Want to fuck you so bad."

Boyd chuckled roughly, his ass clenching in anticipation. "I want that, too."

"You a switch?" Mycroft asked bluntly.

Nodding, Boyd confirmed, "I am. You?"

Mycroft jerked a nod, his fingers tightening on Boyd's shoulders when he gave him a little extra squeeze. "Yessss," he hissed. "But, gods, you better stop that, or I'm gonna blow again."

Grinning, Boyd eased his grip from Mycroft's groin. "Well, we wouldn't want that." Hearing his shifter's groan of dis-may, he quickly snatched up the lube packet. "I'll stretch quick. Want you to give it to me hard and fast, beloved. Wanna feel you deep."

"I can do that," Mycroft agreed, his voice throaty, deepen-ing with his need. "Hurry. I'll stretch you next time."

Boyd nodded, on board with that. He quickly tore open the packet and poured most of the lube onto his fingers. Turning so his hand wasn't in the spray, Boyd rested his free hand on the wall while reaching behind himself.

With skill born of decades of practice, Boyd shoved first one finger, then a second into his ass. He stretched himself swiftly, and soon he had three fingers buried inside him. As he finger-fucked himself, Boyd looked over to see Mycroft staring at him intently. His shifter had his fingers around the base of his prick, obviously doing what he could to keep from coming.

Deciding he was ready, Boyd pulled his fingers free. "Use the rest of the lube, and get in me," he ordered huskily. Resting his weight on both forearms, Boyd jutted out his ass. "Need you, beloved."

Mycroft groaned as he grabbed the lube packet. "Oh, Boyd," he muttered, slathering the slick onto his long, slender shaft. "You're so sensual. So perfect." Easing behind Boyd, Mycroft tossed the empty packet to the floor of the shower before resting his now-free hand on his back. He rubbed up and down his spine as he pressed his dick's head to Boyd's prepared entrance. "And now, you're all mine."

Without a word of warning, Mycroft thrust, sinking deep into Boyd's body in one long, smooth glide.

Boyd arched his back further as he pushed out, accepting his beloved's intrusion, welcoming it. His channel easily stretched to accommodate his shifter's girth, and he relished the feel of his fated match taking him. When Mycroft slid across his prostate, he groaned huskily and whispered his name.

"Such beautiful sounds you make," Mycroft whispered into his ear. Wrapping his arms around Boyd's waist, he paused, their bodies flushed together from thigh to shoulder, his erection sunk deep inside Boyd's body. Mycroft's warm breath ghosted over the sensitive hairs under Boyd's ear as he crooned, "Love hearing you cry my name. My mate. My forever."

"Mycroft," Boyd murmured again. Turning his head, he nuzzled his beloved's temple. "Please, my beloved," he urged. "Please fuck me."

"Fuck now," Mycroft agreed, beginning to ease his erection out of Boyd's body. "Will explore and love on you later, my mate."

Then Mycroft switched directions, slamming into Boyd's body. He began a punishing rhythm, pounding into him over and over. With each pass, Mycroft teased over his prostate — over and over — sending tendrils of fiery pleasure to course through Boyd's veins.

"Yessss," Boyd hissed, reveling in the feel of Mycroft's taking. Arching, he rocked back into each rut. Boyd clenched and released his chute muscles, milking his beloved's erection to the best of his abilities.

Mycroft moaned Boyd's name, the sound one of rapture that pushed Boyd's own need even higher.

"Come in me," Boyd demanded, needing their bond more than he needed his next breath. "Give in." Even though he was the bottom this round, Boyd demanded the control. "Fill me with your seed. Complete us."

Boyd could think of nothing he'd ever wanted more.

To Boyd's dismay, Mycroft's strokes slowed. He groaned in frustration before feeling his shifter's petting hands glide over his rib cage. Mycroft rubbed his cheek against Boyd's neck as he began long-dicking him in slow, steady strokes.

Then . . . Mycroft began to purr.

The vibrating sensation caused goose bumps to erupt on Boyd's arms and legs, the hairs standing on end. Mycroft's fingers found Boyd's nipples, and he plucked at his distended buds. Boyd's gut clenched, and he felt his balls tingle and tighten.

With a gasp, Boyd realized he was about to come again, without a touch to his cock.

"Do it," Mycroft urged. "Come for me, my mate. Come for me, and I will fill your chute with my seed, bonding us for eternity."

Boyd wouldn't have been able to stop himself even if he tried . . . which he didn't. With a roar of bliss, he gave in to his need and came. His orgasm swamped his senses in a rush of heat and ecstasy.

An instant later, Boyd felt it. Mycroft buried his erection deep inside him, clutching him tightly, as he poured his seed within him. Boyd hummed at the feel of his beloved coating his channel with his hot seed.

When Mycroft again sank his teeth into his neck, Boyd groaned with pleasure. He couldn't fight the trembling or the black spots dancing across his vision. Never in Boyd's wildest dreams could he have imagined the bliss of claiming, and how it rocked his world.

In the next instant, Boyd blacked out.

CHAPTER FIVE

When Boyd's body sagged within his hold, they both nearly went down. Mycroft managed to shift his feet and slap a hand to the wall just in time to catch them. Holding tight to his vampire's body, Mycroft steadied them, taking a moment to catch his breath.

Mycroft breathed in the scents of his vampire, arousal, sex, and seed, relishing the fragrant aroma caused by their love-making.

As Mycroft eased his softening prick from Boyd's body, being careful to keep his vampire upright, never before had he been so grateful for shifter strength. After turning off the water, he swept the slightly larger man into his arms and made his way out of the shower. Grabbing a couple of towels as he passed them, Mycroft made his way to the bedroom.

After placing Boyd on the comforter, Mycroft made quick work of drying himself. He tossed the towel in the direction of the bathroom before using the second to dry Boyd, doing a much more thorough job. Then he exited the room and headed to the mini-fridge, fishing out two of the bottles of water that he and Dakota had put in there earlier. Mycroft cracked one and drank half the contents before closing it again.

Returning to Boyd, Mycroft smiled at the picture he made. His vampire's boy-next-door features were relaxed in a half-smile, and his body appeared to glow from a mixture of their passion and the hot water. He'd stretched out an arm at one point, as if searching for Mycroft, even in sleep.

"Stop staring and come to bed."

Okay. Not asleep.

When Boyd cracked open an eyelid and peered up at him, Mycroft smiled. "Would you like some water?" He held out the full bottle. "I found our calisthenics made me thirsty."

Grunting, Boyd pushed to a sitting position before taking it. "Thanks."

Mycroft pulled back the comforter as much as possible with Boyd still sitting on it. After easing under the blanket, he finished his own water before setting the bottle on the nightstand. Then Mycroft relaxed on the bed, watching Boyd drain his own water bottle.

Once Boyd had set the empty on the nightstand, his vampire slipped under the comforter and reclined next to him. He rested his head on Mycroft's shoulder and slung an arm around his waist and one leg over his thighs. With a sigh, Boyd relaxed.

"Goodnight, my mate," Mycroft murmured, turning his head and pecking a kiss to Boyd's lips.

Boyd smiled. "Goodnight, beloved."

Mycroft let out a sigh of his own as he closed his eyes, letting sleep take him.

Everything else could wait until tomorrow.

The trill of a cell phone tugged at Mycroft's subconsciousness. Upon hearing a groan and feeling Boyd ease away from him, he forced open his eyelids. He enjoyed the view as he watched his mate ease from the bed and pad to the bathroom.

Seeing Boyd bend over to retrieve his jeans caused Mycroft's morning wood to harden further. He pushed down the comforter and gripped his length, giving it a few loose tugs for stimulation.

Boyd turned as he answered the phone. "Hello, Master Jaymes." Meeting Mycroft's gaze, his vampire's eyes widened before heat entered them. "Yes, Master. I apologize for not calling last night. I met my beloved last night and ended up a little distracted." Slowly, Boyd stalked toward the bed, his attention riveted on where Mycroft pleasured himself. "Thank you, sir. A shifter. No, sir. Not a cougar." With a chuckle, Boyd murmured, "No, not a rogue, either." Grimacing, he turned his back on Mycroft, obviously attempting to focus on his master's call. "His name is Mycroft Portent. He's an enforcer for the Shifter Council. He's one of the two who are here to review Alpha Forest's behavior." Boyd paused again before he stated, sounding somewhat subdued, "No, Master Jaymes. We haven't talked about the future, yet. We bonded last night and passed out. Your call woke us." Boyd paused again. "Thank you for understanding, Master, but he has a job to do, too, so I'm sure I'll be back at the coven to handle my normal afternoon ride duties." With the way Boyd rubbed the back of his neck, Mycroft admired the play of muscle on his arm. "Yes, I'd be honored to introduce you, Master." Boyd turned back to Mycroft and lowered the phone. "Will you be available to join us for dinner, Mycroft? Master Jaymes would like to meet you."

Mycroft nodded. "Of course, my mate." With a smile, he admitted, "I'd intended to request a formal meeting with your master, anyway, since he's the one who filed the complaint. I'd also like a chance to talk to Lorain about the alpha's treatment of her."

Boyd nodded as he relayed Mycroft's answer. After exchanging a few more words, Boyd hung up. He pinned a feral gaze on Mycroft as he placed the phone on the nightstand.

"You were very distracting, my beloved," Boyd crooned. "Is there something you need?"

Smirking at Boyd, Mycroft returned his hand to his straining erection. "Indeed, there is."

Glancing from Mycroft's face to his dick and back again, Boyd narrowed his eyes and tilted his head. "Hmmm . . . let's see if we can't do something about that."

Except, then Boyd turned and headed to the bathroom.

Mycroft nearly called after him, but his mate returned almost immediately, a small bottle in hand.

Holding it up, Boyd stated, "Lotion. Not the best, but it'll do."

Grinning, Mycroft nodded. "Indeed, it will."

As if that was all the permission Boyd needed, his vampire rejoined him on the bed. He crawled toward Mycroft and inserted a knee between his thighs. Mycroft spread his legs willingly, lifting his arms and welcoming his lover.

"Good morning, beloved," Boyd crooned.

Right before Boyd sealed his lips over Mycroft's own, Mycroft murmured, "Good morning, mate."

Few words were needed for some time after that.

Deliciously sore in all the right places, Mycroft pulled on a pair of jeans. He watched Boyd tug on his only other clean ones and felt grateful that they were roughly the same size. He would end up needing to borrow some of his mate's things. Otherwise, he would need to hit a laundromat.

"You look good in my clothes," Mycroft stated, feeling a primitive thrill upon seeing his mate in his jeans.

Boyd grinned as he pulled on his shirt from the night before. "Thanks. They're comfortable." He folded his soiled jeans and shoved them into the plastic ice bucket bag. Next, Boyd grabbed Mycroft's clothes and shoved them in there, too. "I'll do laundry at the ranch."

"Thank you." That solved one of Mycroft's problems. "Where do you want to eat?"

"There's a diner around the corner," Boyd told him. "One of those chain ones that serve breakfast all day. We can walk to it."

"Sounds fantastic," Mycroft replied.

They'd whiled away nearly the entire morning in bed together. Only the growling of their stomachs had chased them from beneath the sheets. At one point, he'd heard Dakota moving around in the outer room, but his fellow enforcer hadn't disturbed them, although the scent of the coffee had been damn tempting.

"Let's see if Dakota left us any coffee," Boyd stated. "I'm due for a cup."

"Me, too," Mycroft agreed.

Mycroft finished dressing and led the way out of the room. He grabbed his boots and settled on the sofa to tug them on. As he did that, he noticed Dakota sitting at the small kitchenette table with his laptop open before him.

"Morning, Dakota," Mycroft greeted.

Dakota glanced at the clock on the wall, then smirked at him. "Afternoon, Mycroft."

Mycroft laughed and shrugged, completely unrepentant for playing hooky for half a day. Hell, it wasn't every day that a shifter found his mate. With that thought, he realized he had a couple of phone calls of his own to make.

"You joining us for a meal?" Mycroft asked as he pulled out his cell phone.

"Sure," Dakota replied. "If you don't mind, anyway."

"Don't mind at all," Boyd told him, picking up the coffee carafe. "How do you like your coffee, Mycroft?"

"Black is fine," Mycroft replied before hitting a button to call Regales.

"Good afternoon, Mycroft," Regales answered on the third ring. "Is everything going smoothly with the cougars?"

Mycroft scoffed softly before answering, "To be honest, not a clue. I'll have to ask Dakota for a report from last night." Before Regales could question him, Mycroft hurried and explained, "I met my mate last night, so I spent the evening with him. We'll go see the cougars this afternoon."

"Congratulations, Mycroft." Regales sounded genuinely happy for him, which didn't surprise Mycroft. "That's fantastic news. Who is he? Human? Something else?"

"A vampire," Mycroft replied. Smiling and murmuring a thank you, he accepted the cup of coffee from his mate. "His name is Boyd Johnson, and he's a member of the coven that reported the cougar alpha's behavior."

"I'm really happy for you," Regales told him. "Everyone should be so blessed as to find their mate." After a second of hesitation, he asked, "Are we losing you to the coven? Please tell me no. You'd be damn hard to replace."

Mycroft met Boyd's gaze, who'd taken a seat beside him. "We haven't discussed it, yet," he admitted, knowing his mate would be able to hear every word they both said. "I'm going to ask him to move to Savannah, but it's something we both have to decide together."

"Yeah, I get it," Regales replied with a hum. "Well, congrats again. I'll post an announcement on the board," he told him, referring to a digital message board that everyone working for the shifter council had access to. "You'll probably receive plenty of congratulation texts soon."

"And a few, I'm so jealous, messages, too," Dakota commented, revealing that he was listening, as well. He grinned at Mycroft. "I know I'll post one."

"Tell Dakota that his time will come," Regales stated. "Have faith."

"I'm trying, Reg." Dakota sounded a little defeated, and even his shoulders slumped a little. "Still trying."

Mycroft rose and crossed to the other shifter. Resting his hand on Dakota's shoulder, he gave it a reassuring squeeze. "Fate is smiling on us again," he commented. "She won't forget you."

Dakota nodded as he smiled back.

"All right," Regales stated. "I'll let you get back to your

mate and your assignment. Congrats again."

"Thank you, Councilman," Mycroft replied. Then he disconnected the call and placed his phone in his pocket. Before Mycroft could think up anything else reassuring to say, his stomach grumbled.

"How about we head to the coven for a meal," Boyd offered. "It's free, and Master Jaymes does want to meet with you."

Mycroft arched one brow at Dakota in silent question.

Dakota rose from his seat as he closed his laptop. "Sounds good to me. I'm always up for a free meal."

After a nod, Mycroft took a deep swallow of his coffee. He was nearly startled when he felt Boyd's arms slide around his waist from behind. He hadn't realized his vampire had moved.

"Hey," Boyd murmured into his ear. "Were you serious about asking me to move?"

Turning his head, Mycroft peered over his shoulder at his mate. "Yes, it's something I'm hoping you'll consider." He met Boyd's blue-eyed gaze and added, "There are other vampires working for the Shifter Council, so you wouldn't be alone there."

Boyd nodded slowly. "It would make sense for me to be the one to move, all things considered." With a small shrug and a grin, he added, "As long as there's somewhere for me to board my horse."

Pleased beyond measure, Mycroft turned in Boyd's embrace and wrapped his arms around him. "We'll find something," he told him before taking his vampire's mouth in a kiss that curled his toes.

CHAPTER SIX

Boyd spotted a number of figures waiting on the porch as Mycroft drove up the driveway. "Huh," he commented over the noise of the engine. "Got a whole welcoming committee."

Mycroft glanced over his shoulder at him before returning his focus to driving. "Probably to offer congratulations," he stated. "Plus, we're from the Shifter Council. Proper etiquette requires a greeting."

"Oh, right." Boyd hadn't thought about that.

Reaching back, Mycroft squeezed Boyd's knee affectionately. "Let's get the formalities out of the way." Then he parked the motorcycle in front of the porch.

Boyd swung off the bike before removing the helmet. After Mycroft had dismounted, he handed it to his beloved. Mycroft smiled his thanks and hung it on a handlebar.

Beside them, Dakota was doing the same.

Leading the way, Boyd headed toward the porch steps. Before he'd reached them, Master Jaymes stepped off the porch. He held out his hand to Mycroft.

"Welcome to my coven, Head Enforcer Mycroft," he stated. "I'm Master Jaymes Martinez. It's an honor to have you."

Mycroft took Master Jaymes's hand, shaking briefly, as he stated, "The honor is mine. Thank you for not only your hospitality, but also for reporting errant shifter behavior." He released him and indicated Dakota. "This is Enforcer Dakota Drudeson. One of our best."

"Welcome, Enforcer Dakota," Master Jaymes repeated,

shaking Dakota's hand.

"Thank you, Master Jaymes," Dakota responded.

Master Jaymes grinned broadly, showing off his fangs. "Allow me to introduce my beloved, Paul, as well as my Second Gypsum, his beloved, Lucius, and my enforcers, Rhyme and Clarice."

Mycroft tipped his chin in a nod to each as they were introduced, as did Dakota.

Once that was done, Master Jaymes grinned once more. "Now that the formalities are out of the way . . ." He turned toward Boyd and drew him into a hug. "Congratulations, Boyd. I'm so very happy for you."

Boyd returned Master Jaymes's quick embrace, smiling widely. "Thank you, Master. I couldn't be happier."

"Glad to hear it," his master replied. "Finding your beloved is a true blessing that I hope all of my vampires can one day enjoy."

"So you have a few more single vampires?" Dakota questioned, stepping forward and resting his hands on his hips. "I'm still looking for my mate." Then the big male waggled his eyebrows. "Although, I hear a vampire's bite is euphoric even if it isn't your mate."

Clarice sauntered closer as she gave Dakota a lascivious once over. "If you want to find out, I'd be happy to assist." Smirking, she added, "It's been quite some time since I've enjoyed shifter blood."

Dakota hummed as he eyed her. "Hmmm, you and I will have to talk later."

Gypsum chuckled as he descended the stairs. "You guys do that. I'm much more interested in your rides," he told them, eyeing the pair of motorcycles. "I know it's bad form to ask to take a guy's bike for a spin, but damn, is it tempting to do so." He stopped next to Mycroft's motorcycle and swept an appreciative touch over the fender. "How fast have you had her?"

"Two-twenty-three on the highway," Mycroft replied, and Gypsum whistled.

Jaymes touched Boyd's upper arm, drawing his attention. "Am I losing you to the Shifter Council?" he asked curiously. "Or haven't you discussed it, yet?"

Boyd nodded. "I think so, Master," he replied. "With Mycroft being the Head Enforcer for them, it makes more sense for me to do the relocating."

With a sigh, Jaymes nodded back. "I figured as much." Holding his gaze, he told him, "Know that you will always have a place here. You both do."

"Thank you, Master," Boyd replied gratefully. Then he turned and un-bungeed the plastic bag of clothes from the back of the bike. "I need to start a load of laundry real quick."

Jaymes stepped back with a nod. "Of course."

Boyd rested his hand on Mycroft's lower back, and his beloved focused on him. "I'm going to start some laundry," he told his shifter. "I'll be right back for that meal."

Mycroft cupped his jaw and pressed a kiss to his lips. "See you soon, my mate."

After another peck, Boyd turned away and hurried into the ranch house, leaving Mycroft chatting about motorcycles with Gypsum. He headed up to his suite and dumped the bag of clothes into his already half-full laundry basket. Picking that up, he strode back downstairs to the basement.

Seven washing machines and dryers had been installed in the expansive space. Placing his basket beside one, he grabbed his choice of detergent—there were six different kinds—and poured a serving into two washing machines. He returned it to the shelf before adding his and Mycroft's clothes to the two washers. Then he checked his watch, noting the time, so he would know when to return and move them to the dryers.

By the time Boyd returned to the main floor, Murdoch was waiting. His friend grabbed him and wrapped him in a tight hug, offering his congratulations. Boyd accepted the embrace, hugging him back.

When Murdoch released him, his smile appeared a little sad. "I'm going to miss you, my friend."

Chuckling softly, Boyd shook his head. "This isn't the end, Murdoch. I'll visit, and I expect you to do the same." He winked while adding, "Besides, you have your own handsome beloved to keep you occupied."

Murdoch nodded. "One of those constants in life. Change."

"Exactly," Boyd agreed. "But in this case, it's a fantastic change."

"Yes, it is. I'm so very happy for you." Murdoch patted him on the shoulder. "So, where is Mycroft, anyway?"

"Probably still out front talking to Gypsum about motorcycles," Boyd told him, turning in that direction.

"Ah." Murdoch nodded. "I came in through the back."

Boyd started that way with Murdoch accompanying him. As he moved, his stomach growled. Rubbing his belly, he anticipated the feast he knew Vaughn would have in the dining hall. Their chef always had plenty of variety.

Murdoch chuckled. "You forget to eat or something?" he teased, obviously having heard Boyd's stomach grumbling.

"Or something," Boyd replied with a smirk.

His eyes widening, Murdoch muttered, "Oh, shit. Did you skip it in favor of fucking?"

Boyd just smiled at his buddy. He had little desire to share the details of his and Mycroft's love-making sessions. His memories were his own.

Murdoch must have realized it, for he didn't press for details. "Well, I'm happy for ya." He patted Boyd on the shoulder even as Boyd's stomach growled again, making him laugh. "But I think we better get something in there before it eats itself."

"I'm definitely ready to eat," Boyd conceded. "I know Mycroft is, too."

Boyd stepped out on the front porch, seeing that Rhyme had left, probably in search of his beloved, Max. When he approached Mycroft's side, the smile he received from his beloved caused his heart to trip wildly in his chest. The kiss Mycroft gave him sent heat firing through his veins once more.

Several wolf whistles rent the air, and they separated with a laugh.

"Let's move this to the dining hall," Jaymes encouraged. With a smirk, he added, "I heard Mycroft's stomach rumble a few times."

Mycroft chuckled as he wrapped his arm around Boyd's waist, and Boyd mirrored the move. The group headed across the yard to the dining hall.

Two hours later, Boyd watched Mycroft's taillights disappear up the driveway. He rubbed at his chest, surprised at the pang he felt there. After spending less than a day with his beloved, Boyd hated that he needed to separate from him.

"It happens fast, doesn't it?" Jaymes commented softly, resting his hand on his shoulder and offering a sympathetic squeeze. "Loving your beloved."

Boyd cocked his head.

Do I love my beloved already?

Huh. I think I do.

"With cheetah speed," Boyd conceded.

"Is that the type of cat he is?" Jaymes asked, using his hold to urge Boyd to turn and head up the stairs. "With the way he'd painted his motorcycle, I did wonder."

"It is," Boyd confirmed. "This driving need to be with him, to watch his back . . . it really crept up on me fast, but I know I can't interfere with his work."

"I know exactly how you feel," Jaymes told him, and Boyd

knew his master did.

Jaymes had needed to wait several months before being able to claim Paul, because when Jaymes had met Paul, the human had been underage. Now that Boyd had met his own beloved, he was wholly impressed with his master's strength of will. Boyd couldn't imagine having had to wait a day to claim Mycroft let alone several months.

"Mycroft gave you a key card to his hotel suite, and he said he would meet you back there this evening," Jaymes reminded him. With a cheeky grin, he asked, "Didn't you tell him that all our suites are sound-proofed?"

Due to so many vampires finding their beloveds coupled with the fact that paranormals had superior hearing, Master Jaymes had sound-proofed every bedroom in the coven house over a decade before.

Boyd chuckled even as he nodded. "Yes. I told him." As he turned toward the stairs that led to the basement, he admitted, "I think it has more to do with protocol, to be honest. He doesn't want to be seen staying at the coven when he's working on a report that we filed."

"Ah, showing no bias." Jaymes nodded. "Understandable. Well, at least you have plenty to keep you occupied until it's time to head out," Jaymes reminded him.

Nodding, Boyd told his master, "I'm going to change the laundry, then get dressed for work." As comfortable as Mycroft's jeans were, they weren't heavy-duty enough for ranch work. Boyd worried he would tear them or something. "Then I'll get out there to saddle the horses for the mid-afternoon trail ride."

"Thank you, Boyd." Jaymes dipped his chin in a nod. "And I'll talk to Mathe about finding you boxes to pack your things."

Boyd thanked his coven master, then headed to change his laundry.

As Boyd worked, whiling away the rest of the day, he appreciated all the well wishes his fellow vampires and their beloveds offered him. After the trail ride, Murdoch and Malakai helped him pack his suite. He stacked the boxes along a wall near the door in preparation of loading them into his truck.

A little after eight, Boyd couldn't wait any longer. He hopped into his vehicle, Mycroft's clean clothes on the seat beside him, and headed to the hotel. When he let himself into the room, the lights were off, and neither Mycroft nor Dakota were there.

Grabbing a beer from the box he'd brought with him, Boyd turned on the TV and settled in to wait.

CHAPTER SEVEN

"That's preposterous," Alpha Forest growled, crossing his arms over his chest. He glared at Mycroft, malice filling his hard brown eyes. "I never kicked out any pride members."

Mycroft ignored the way the alpha straightened to his full height of six-foot-three and tried to intimidate him with his larger stature. He'd taken down bear shifters to win his position. The cougar was nothing. Besides, Mycroft knew Dakota would have his back in a fight.

Standing inside Alpha Forest's study with Beta Bradley, Enforcer Parakesh, and Enforcer Khan, Mycroft kept his gaze steady on the alpha. "Lorain Caldsyn was part of your pride until recently, was she not?"

Rolling his eyes, Forest sneered at him. "This is about Lorain? She's human," he stated dismissively. "She was never part of my pride."

"According to our report, Lorain's mother was the fated mate of Niall, one of your cougar shifters, correct?" Mycroft pressed.

"Exactly, Lorain's mother, Gracie," Forest stated, as if that statement made his point.

"And Gracie bonded with Niall twenty-four years ago when Lorain was two years old," Mycroft continued calmly. "Niall raised Lorain as his own, and there were no other children from the union." Before Forest could counter him again, Mycroft continued, "For twenty-four years, Lorain lived under your care, Alpha Forest, as one of your members."

Forest's face began to darken as his anger obviously

surged. The peppery scent started to fill the room. His cougar inner circle shifted in obvious discomfort, and the two enforcers exchanged covert glances.

"If I want to run a useless human out of my territory because she couldn't pay her rent," Forest began with a growl in his voice. "Then that's my business." He pointed his finger at Mycroft and stated belligerently, "And no damn council enforcer is going to make me offer restitution to a stupid hussy who couldn't keep her legs closed and ended up knocked up by a vampire." With a scoff and a wave of his hand as if shooing away a fly, Forest continued, "She's their problem now. Good riddance."

"I understand Niall and Gracie did not pay rent when they were living," Mycroft stated, keeping his voice even. "And Lorain had remained in that family home after their passing six months ago?"

"So." A muscle ticked in Forest's jaw.

"You asked for monthly rent of twelve-hundred dollars from Lorain less than a week after the funeral for her parents," Mycroft stated, allowing a bit of chill to fill his voice. "Not a week in the grave, and you were demanding money from her in order to stay in her own home."

"It wasn't her home," Forest barked. "It's a pride home."

"According to our traditions, Lorain was pride until she chose to leave," Mycroft told Alpha Forest. "Therefore, you will reimburse her the five months of rent she paid you. You will also pay a restitution equal to five years' worth of rent to cover emotional grief and trauma." While Mycroft didn't need to check his math, he still glanced at his phone, just because he knew the blatant disrespect would irritate the asshole alpha. "That comes to seventy-eight thousand dollars. You have two weeks to give it to her, or you will be removed as alpha."

"Seventy-eight thousand," Enforcer Parakesh whispered,

shock filling his tone. He glanced between Khan and Bradley. "How can we possibly come up with that?"

"I told you," Forest roared, stalking forward. "I ain't givin' Lorain a bleedin' cent, and there ain't nothin' you can do about it." Raising his hand in a fist threateningly, he growled, "She wasn't my responsibility and never was. Now get the fuck out of my lands, or you'll be sorry."

"I would reconsider your actions, Alpha Forest." Dakota stepped forward, his voice holding a deadly serious note. "Before you do something that can't be resolved with restitution."

Threatening a Shifter Council representative carried a heavy restitution penalty. If a representative was attacked, they were within their right to use lethal force to protect themselves. The life of whoever gave the order to attack was forfeit as well.

Forest's face darkened further, and his nostrils flared. He clenched his jaw so hard Mycroft could hear his teeth grinding.

In all honesty, Mycroft really hoped that Forest took a swing at him. He hadn't issued a good beatdown in decades.

"Alpha Forest, I challenge you for the right to lead the pride."

Arching one brow, betraying his surprise, Mycroft saw Beta Bradley step forward. He spotted the way both enforcers' jaws sagged open. Forest's eyes widened as he snapped his attention to his beta.

"What the fuck?" Forest demanded. "You can't challenge me."

"He can, and he just did." Dakota's voice held a definite hint of amusement. "Does your pride have a fighting ring?"

"There ain't gonna be no fight," Forest thundered, pinning a feral glare on Bradley. "Is there, *Beta*."

Beta Bradley straightened his shoulders, refusing to back

down. "Sorry, Alpha Forest, but I think this is the wake-up call that I've needed." His fingers twitched at his sides, as if he struggled not to ball them into fists. "I should have done it when you started charging Lorain rent."

Enforcer Khan answered Dakota's question. "Yes, Enforcer Dakota. We have a fighting ring," he told them. "It's out back."

"If you will secure Alpha Forest," Mycroft ordered Dakota. "I'll inspect the ring." He turned his attention to Enforcer Parakesh. "Please spread the word to every pride member in the area. There will be a Fight for Position challenge in one hour."

Forest roared and lunged at Mycroft, but Dakota stepped forward and intervened. He grabbed the male's wrist and swung him around to face the wall. With quick, efficient moves, Dakota secured Forest's hands behind his back, clamping on a pair of specially designed, reinforced cuffs.

Dakota arched one brow as he peered over his shoulder at Mycroft. "Is the fight still on, or was that enough to arrest him and send him to Shifter Headquarters?"

Mycroft heaved a deep sigh, grimacing. "You should have let him take a swing at me," he grumbled, crossing his arms over his chest. Turning, Mycroft focused on Bradley. "What would you prefer?"

Bradley rubbed his jaw. "Well, the transition of leadership to me would go smoother if I beat him in the ring," he admitted. "That's how we've been running the pride for the last century, so that's what our people will expect." With a shrug, Bradley added, "It's our way."

"As you wish," Mycroft responded. "Do you have a secure place for us to hold him until the fight?"

"You bastards," Forest snarled, glaring at his enforcers. "When I'm finished with Bradley, you're all out of your positions. I'm going to recruit a whole new inner circle." His eyes took on a maniacal glow as Forest added, "Then no one will stand in my way of taking out that fucking coven."

Tipping his head back, Bradley groaned. "Why the hell would you want to take out the coven?" He frowned at Forest. "We have plenty of land to run, and we're self-sufficient."

"After the vampires are gone, I'll take over Amarillo," Forest continued as if Bradley hadn't spoken. "Then —"

"And we've heard enough of your bullshit plans," Dakota grumbled, shoving a sock into Forest's mouth.

Mycroft watched in surprise as Dakota slid his bare foot back into his motorcycle boot. How or when the big shifter had managed to remove the heavy footwear while still holding Forest, he had no idea. Barking a laugh, Mycroft couldn't help his amusement upon seeing Forest's shocked expression at finding a dirty sock in his mouth.

If looks could kill.

Fortunately, they couldn't.

"Okay," Mycroft rumbled, turning his attention back to the others. "You'd better win, Bradley."

Otherwise, Mycroft would end up having to assign an investigator to keep track of Forest's actions.

Huh. I probably should anyway, regardless of what happens. This shifter is nuts.

"I'll win," Bradley told him confidently, leading the way from the study. "Forest doesn't keep up on his training."

Keeping his thoughts to himself, Mycroft followed. Dakota followed Bradley with Forest in tow. Bradley explained that there were detention cells beneath the house.

Mycroft followed Khan while Parakesh pulled out his phone and made a call. He hoped the enforcer was doing as he requested and rounding up as many members as possible. They needed a good viewing for Bradley's take-over.

Khan led Mycroft around the main house to a well-worn path leading into the trees. His phone vibrated in his pocket, drawing his attention. He pulled it out and smiled, seeing a text from Boyd.

Thinking of you. Do you ride horses? We could bring a second horse from the ranch.

Warmth settled in Mycroft's gut as he shot off a quick response, all the while continuing to glance at Khan, following him.

It's been years, but I'd love to ride with you. Pick out a friendly one for me.

After a couple of seconds, Mycroft sent a second message.

This is going to take a little longer than I thought, but I hope to still be back at the hotel by nightfall. Looking forward to seeing you, my mate.

Me, too. Stay safe.

Always.

With that final message, Mycroft returned his phone to his jeans' pocket.

After a few minute hike, Mycroft entered a huge clearing. He swept his gaze over the area, nodding absently. The space was easily fifty yards in diameter. Grass grew in sparse clumps throughout the middle of the area, with most of it on the outer edges before reaching the trees.

"Perfect," Mycroft murmured, turning his attention to Khan. "Guess you guys issue a lot of challenges."

Khan nodded. "Yes, sir."

"How many members do you expect to show up on such short notice?" Mycroft asked curiously. According to his records, the pride should have consisted in the number of low thirties.

"Probably a couple dozen," Khan told him. "About a dozen people are in town working. The rest work the gardens, the fields, and tend our goat herds."

"Perfect."

True to Khan's predication, within the hour, nearly two dozen people milled around the edges of the circle.

Mycroft swept his gaze over the assembled people. There were several mothers with a half-dozen children. A number of older men wore dirty jeans, as if they'd just come in from the fields. Another group of men who appeared younger eyed Mycroft with distrust.

He figured that was to be expected, all things considered.

Enforcer Khan stepped into the circle as Dakota brought a still cuffed Forest to the clearing. Bradley moved to the opposite side of the circle, removed his shirt, and kicked off his shoes. As Bradley unbuttoned his pants and toed off his socks, Khan raised his hands, calling for silence, not that very many people had been talking.

"Today, Beta Bradley has challenged Alpha Forest for the right to lead our pride," Khan announced, sweeping his gaze over the assembled group. A few murmurs went through the crowd, but they were quickly drowned out by Khan saying, "The challenge is to submission. The losing party will have to leave pride lands within an hour." Indicating Mycroft and Dakota, Khan added, "The challenge is being presided over by Shifter Council Enforcers Mycroft and Dakota." Then he focused on Dakota. "Please release Alpha Forest, so he may shift for the fight."

While clearly reluctant, Dakota did it. He took the sock from Forest's mouth first, then opened the cuffs and took a step backward.

Forest immediately spun and snarled, "You'll pay for this. You'll *all* pay for this."

Mycroft just resisted rolling his eyes.

"Alpha Forest," Khan called, doing his best to remain stoic. "Your challenger awaits you, sir."

Forest panned his gaze around the assembled group, who all watched him expectantly. He must have realized there was no getting out of it, for he grabbed the hem of his shirt and whipped it over his head. As Forest kicked off his shoes and unbuttoned his jeans, he pinned Bradley with an angry look.

"Traitor," Forest taunted, curling his lip. "I'm going to tear your hide from your body."

Then Forest began to shift, not seeming to care that he still wore his jeans and socks.

Bradley shoved out of his own pants and started his own shift.

Even before Forest had completely attained his cougar form, he began moving awkwardly toward Bradley, his clothes falling from his body. To Bradley's credit, he didn't seem worried. Instead, he focused on his shift, allowing him to complete it before Forest could even get close.

Taking advantage, Bradley lunged at Forest, and the fight was on.

CHAPTER EIGHT

The click of the hotel room door's locks roused Boyd. The TV was still playing, although it was something he didn't recognize. The room was mostly dark, illuminated only by a small lamp on the end table. He guessed he'd been asleep for over an hour.

Turning his head, Boyd watched the door open, light spilling in from the hallway. He recognized Mycroft's leaner frame followed by Dakota's larger one. His beloved's scent reached him just as Mycroft spotted him. Boyd didn't know if it was his beloved's alluring aroma or if it was the man's relieved, welcoming smile, but his pulse quickly sped up in his veins.

"Hi, beloved," Boyd greeted, rising to his feet and opening his arms. "Missed you."

Mycroft immediately accepted his embrace, wrapping him in his arms.

Tipping his head, Boyd captured his beloved's mouth in a heartfelt kiss. He hummed appreciatively upon tasting the shifter's unique flavor. Tightening his arms, Boyd clutched Mycroft close, flushing their bodies.

Boyd registered the flare of light, telling him Dakota had turned on a lamp. With his eyes closed and his senses surrounded by his beloved, he couldn't give a shit that the man was there. He took his time mapping Mycroft's mouth, and his beloved let him, seeming to be happy to follow his lead.

When breathing became paramount, Boyd finally lifted his head, parting their lips. He gasped, sucking in a much-needed lungful of air. To his delight, Boyd saw that Mycroft was in much the same situation, his chest expanding swiftly as he breathed.

Mycroft found his voice first, murmuring, "Missed you, too."

Grinning, Boyd told him, "Good. Means you'll always hurry back to me as swiftly as possible."

"That I will."

"You hungry, Boyd? We brought pizza," Dakota cut in. "And got any more of that beer? Otherwise, I'll open the carton we just brought." With a deep sigh, Dakota grumbled, "After the asshole we had to deal with today, I totally want one."

Finally, the scent of pepperoni, marinara, and cheese registered to Boyd's senses. "Yeah." His mouth watered for a new reason. "I could eat." Picking up the mostly full twelve-pack with one hand, Boyd wrapped his other arm around Mycroft and started toward the table. He just couldn't seem to stop touching his lover. "Here. Help yourself."

Boyd placed the box on the table next to the stack of three extra-large pizzas. "What kind did you get?" Then he squeezed Mycroft's hip before pecking a kiss to his neck. "You smell better than the pizza."

Mycroft chuckled even as he eased from Boyd's grip. "Glad to hear it," he stated with a wink. "Are there paper plates or something in these cupboards?"

Then Mycroft began rummaging, obviously intent on answering his own question.

"We have a three-meat, a double pepperoni, and a chicken alfredo," Dakota told him, opening each in turn. "And of course" — he waggled his eyebrows — "all have extra cheese."

"And you got it from *Geppetto's*. Awesome," Boyd commented, noticing the logo on the boxes. "They're the best around here."

"Really?" Mycroft returned with three plastic plates, which he set on the table.

Boyd grabbed a plate after Dakota did as he nodded. "Yep. In my opinion, anyway." With a smirk, he added, "If you ask Murdoch, he'll tell you the best is *Mama Ria's*, but he's totally wrong."

The other men laughed, and they all took a seat at the table.

"So, an asshole, huh?" Boyd grabbed a slice from each pie, loading up his plate. "I'm assuming you're talking about Alpha Forest because the few times I've talked to Bradley in a bar, he seemed to be a decent sort."

"Yep." Dakota smirked. "And he's not alpha anymore. Bradley is."

"Really?" Boyd didn't bother trying to hide his surprise. Before taking a big bite of his double pepperoni slice, he stated, "I didn't realize you were going to roust the douche."

After swallowing a bite of chicken alfredo, Mycroft admitted, "We hadn't intended to. After talking with Lorain at your coven house this afternoon, we'd only planned to lay out guidelines for his restitution." Twisting his lips into a grimace as he shook his head, Mycroft told him, "Let's just say, Forest was none-too-pleased, and he started to threaten us."

Dakota snorted. "Bad move."

"With your jobs, you probably get threatened a lot." Boyd hadn't really thought about it before, but upon hearing the tale, he worried for his beloved's safety. "I mean, you're constantly going into random packs and prides with the intention of disrupting them in some way."

"True," Dakota confirmed with a nod. "But there are steep penalties in place for those who threaten or attack a council representative." Smirking, Dakota explained, "Heavy restitution all the way up to death. It's a big no-no."

"Oh." Boyd took another bite of his pizza, relishing the flavors exploding on his tongue. Hearing that made him feel a bit better about his beloved's job.

"Anyway." Mycroft picked up the tale. "Bradley must have realized that Forest was becoming unhinged, so he challenged him for his position." With a snicker, he stated, "Bradley took him out in about two minutes."

"Makes me wonder why Bradley didn't do it sooner," Dakota mused, tossing his crust onto his plate in favor of a fresh three-meat slice. "Guess maybe Forest wasn't always that bad."

"The aftermath is what took so long," Mycroft griped, sporting an apologetic look. "After Forest submitted, he went after Bradley again. That didn't work. Then he went after me. Bradley stopped him again. Then he got away from the pride enforcers and came after me once more." Mycroft scowled at Dakota. "I wish you would stop interfering. I wanted to kick his ass."

Dakota shrugged his wide shoulders, not looking at all repentant. "Just doing my job."

"Anyway, Dakota shifted, shredding his clothes, and caught Forest's cougar in his mouth." Mycroft laughed as he shook his head. "Really put the fear of god into the moron. Even pissed himself."

"That almost got in my mouth, by the way." Dakota scowled as he used his pizza to point at Mycroft. "Not funny."

Unable to help himself, Boyd focused on Dakota. "What are you?"

Grinning broadly, Dakota replied, "Komodo dragon. I'm a big ass fucker."

"Damn," Boyd whispered, impressed. "Komodo dragon. Never thought about those being shifters."

"Wait until you see a *real* dragon," Mycroft quipped with a wink. "Now *those* are big ass fuckers."

Boyd's jaw sagged open as he stared at Mycroft wide-eyed. "Are you serious?" he asked once he'd managed to close his mouth. "Dragons? Like, for real? There are *real* dragon shifters. Breathing fire dragons?"

"Some of them," Mycroft confirmed. "Others breathe ice. Some can control an element, like earth or wind." Then he shrugged as he wiggled his hand in a *so-so* gesture. "There's debate about whether dragons are truly shifters because they're tied so closely with the elements."

"And they're magick," Dakota told him with a shrug. "And if I ever met one, I didn't know it." Cocking his head, he focused on Mycroft. "Anyone I know?"

Mycroft opened his mouth, then shut it again. For a second, he looked conflicted. Then he heaved a sigh and pointed at Dakota. "You can't say a word. Not even to your brothers. Understand?"

"Yeah, yeah." Dakota leaned forward, eagerness lighting his green eyes.

Hell, he practically looks like he's salivating.

Grimacing, Mycroft added, "And you can't approach him. I only know because I'm Head Enforcer."

"Okay." Dakota nodded. "Which enforcer?"

Mycroft shook his head. "Not an enforcer. It's Charon."

"Charon?" Dakota appeared confused for a second. Then his eyes widened comically. "Charon, the dishwasher? That Charon?"

Nodding once, Mycroft picked up a piece of three-meat pizza. "Yep."

Dakota's brows furrowed, and the scent of his confusion flooded the area. "But . . . he's a human."

Chuckling, Mycroft chewed and swallowed. "That's what he wants people to think. He's actually our liaison between the Shifter Council and the dragons." With a shrug, he added, "He cloaks his scent."

"You did say they were magick," Boyd pointed out.

"Damn," Dakota whispered, clearly shell-shocked. "Little Charon is a dragon shifter."

Mycroft groaned as he waggled his head back and forth a little. "Not so little, actually," he revealed with a grimace. "He glamours his form, too." With a deep sigh, Mycroft muttered, "I knew I shouldn't have said anything."

"Wow, I—" Dakota paused and shook his head once. He stared at his pizza slice for a couple of heartbeats before he muttered, "Just wow." Then Dakota shoved the food into his mouth, clearly at a loss for words.

Boyd didn't know what to say, either. After all, dragons were real. He'd only recently learned that angels were real, too. There was still so much out there for him to learn.

"Anyway." Mycroft shrugged. "Forest is sitting in the cougar's lock-up beneath their main house. We're on motorcycles, so we're not equipped to transport him." Grimacing, Mycroft glanced around with a frown. "I should really find my tablet so I can figure out a team to come get him."

"It's probably still in your duffle bag," Dakota teased around a mouthful of food.

Mycroft scoffed. "You're probably right." With a wink, he told Boyd, "We had a race to get here, although we really never left each other's sides too much. First one in the parking lot got to choose the rooms." He used his piece of pizza to indicate the doors of the bedrooms in the two-room suite. "Of course, both of them look about the same."

Dakota shrugged. "Mine has a jetted tub instead of a massive shower, so I don't mind."

Boyd nodded. The mention of the enormous shower reminded him of all the fun they'd had in it, so he appreciated that Mycroft ended up with it. Except—"Who won?"

With a smug smile, Mycroft raised his hand. After swallowing some pizza, he stated, "We used a lot of back roads and still turned the twenty-plus hour trip from Savannah into just under nine hours." Winking, he claimed, "Only stopped for fuel."

"And drove on those racing machines like bats out of hell," Boyd guessed.

With a laugh, Dakota nodded. "It was fun."

Mycroft made a noise of agreement. "But now it means we have to wait for others to transport Forest."

"Do you think I could help?" Boyd offered. "I'm going to be pulling a horse trailer. We could always truss him up and stick him in the tack room. Then you guys ride as guards."

Dakota laughed again. "I love that idea." With a grin, he stated, "Let's do it."

"We'll have to make certain you don't get pulled over," Mycroft stated, an amused smile teasing at the corners of his lips. "After all, that would be damn hard to explain."

Boyd tapped the side of his head. "Vampire, remember? I'll just trance the cop. Easy peasy."

Mycroft hummed, pinning a heated look on Boyd. "Easy peasy. I like it."

Feeling his blood heat from that look, Boyd grinned. "So glad I can help."

"Aaaand, on that note." Dakota stood and began putting a couple of slices from the other pizzas into the one with the three-meat. "I'll just take this into my room, with my case of beer, and turn up my TV really loud."

Then the other shifter did just that.

As Boyd followed Mycroft into their own room, he would have felt bad about running Dakota off . . . except, then he had his beloved in his arms and could think of nothing but getting them both naked as swiftly as possible.

CHAPTER NINE

"Well, that was awful nice of Jaymes to lend us an SUV," Dakota rumbled as he relaxed in the high-end vehicle's passenger seat. He smirked at Mycroft. "What'd you think of that cute bay horse Boyd picked out for you?"

Mycroft smiled at the memory. "The gelding is sweet," he stated as he recalled the horse. Just as he'd requested, Boyd had found a friendly, well-trained mount for him. The horse had even come running when Boyd had whistled. "It's been a while since I've ridden," Mycroft admitted. "But it's one of my vampire's passions, so I don't mind taking it up again."

"We shifters do like to do whatever we can to make our mates happy," Dakota stated sagely. Then he sighed and grumbled, "Not that I know anything about that."

"You will," Mycroft told him, reaching over to pat his shoulder. "Fate's started smiling on us. Your turn will come."

"From your lips to Fate's ears," Dakota stated with a smile.

The pair fell silent as they made the turn onto pride lands. Mycroft peered left and right, taking in the area. Several people working in the fields waved, clearly pleased to see them, so both he and Dakota waved back.

"They look happier," Dakota commented softly.

Mycroft nodded in agreement. "Yeah, they do." Glancing around, he murmured, "I wonder how long Forest has been slowly losing his sanity."

"Tough to say," Dakota replied with a shake of his head. "At least things will get better for them now. I like Bradley."

"May the power *not* go to his head," Mycroft murmured.

As seen by Forest's decline, some shifters just couldn't handle power.

"I think he'll be okay," Dakota repeated softly.

Then Mycroft turned the vehicle into the drive before the main lodge. He spotted Alpha Bradley on the porch along with his enforcers. Mycroft absently wondered who the man would choose as the new beta. From his conversations with both men, each seemed to have their strengths and would probably make good right-hand men.

"I don't envy him his choice," Dakota muttered, and Mycroft jerked a nod, silently agreeing with him.

After shutting off the SUV, Mycroft grabbed his door handle and exited. He moved to the front, finding Dakota falling into step right next to him. The Komodo shifter dragon certainly knew his job.

"Okay, Dakota," Mycroft muttered. "Let's get this done."

"Yep," Dakota grunted.

"Enforcer Mycroft," Alpha Bradley greeted with a smile and a dip of his head. "Welcome back." Then his expression sobered. "Thank you for taking Forest so swiftly. He's . . ." Bradley's voice trailed off, and he grimaced. "Well, you can imagine."

"I can indeed." Mycroft had taken in many belligerent crazy shifters over the decades, although it'd been a few years since he'd done fieldwork. With a tight smile, he assured, "We'll take him off your hands, and you won't have to worry about him again."

"Thank you," Bradley repeated. Then he turned and began leading through the house. Khan and Parakesh fell into step around them.

"Have you had any trouble with those under you?" Dakota asked, peering around the quiet house.

Bradley shrugged, glancing over his shoulder at them. "Two left the pride instead of accepting me as their alpha. A couple more did it grudgingly," he admitted. "Most everyone else didn't have a problem with the change." Scoffing, Bradley admitted, "Hell, most I met with scented of being happy about it." He shook his head. "Don't know why I didn't realize it sooner."

"They were good at hiding their concern," Khan stated quietly. "They didn't bring it to us."

"Probably because they thought we were cut from the same crazy cloth as Forest," Parakesh grumbled, a frown furrowing his brows. "We all should have had a pow-wow a *long* time ago."

Bradley dipped his head in a nod of acknowledgment, but he didn't bother commenting.

Mycroft got it. Sometimes, when you were close to it, you couldn't always see the problem until a catalyst forced you to notice. He'd seen it countless times.

Reaching the holding cells, Mycroft watched as Parakesh opened the door. He found himself surprised when Forest didn't immediately attack. Instead, they found him sitting quietly in the cells, glaring daggers at them.

After exchanging a glance with Dakota, Mycroft dipped his chin in a nod. His fellow enforcer headed into the cell, cuffs in hand. The Komodo dragon shifter wore a pair of sweatpants, a t-shirt, and sandals, just in case he needed to shift again.

Except, that didn't seem to be necessary.

With a haughty look, Forest rose to his feet. He even turned around and placed his hands behind him. While he scented of rage, Forest didn't make a move against them.

Mycroft forced down his unease, unwilling to allow the scent to permeate the room. Just because he didn't trust Forest's sudden acquiescence didn't mean he wanted anyone else to know. Instead, Mycroft stepped out of the room and offered Dakota plenty of space to guide their prisoner.

"Time to go," Dakota muttered, pushing the other shifter

before him.

With a curl of his lip and a hate-filled glare at all those around him, Forest obeyed, moving out of the cell.

Dakota guided Forest up the stairs and out of the house. After double-checking the cuffs, he helped him into one of the middle captain's chairs. Then Dakota climbed in next to him.

Mycroft turned back to Bradley. "If you need anything, don't be afraid to call." Then he held out a card to the shifter, giving the male his office line and cell number.

"Thank you," Bradley replied with a nod of acceptance.

After one more nod, Mycroft rounded the SUV and climbed behind the wheel. He brought the vehicle rumbling to life. A glance behind him confirmed the space was clear, so he shifted into reverse and started them on their journey out of pride territory.

Glancing in the rearview mirror, Mycroft took in Forest's stony visage. He peered out the window without saying a word, a muscle ticking in his clenched jaw. Mycroft glanced over his shoulder and arched a brow, but Dakota's hard expression told him the other shifter was feeling the same — concerned.

Mycroft bit back a sigh, unwilling to let Forest know of his concern. Instead, he focused on driving. He sped up, wanting to get to the coven as swiftly as possible.

Thirty minutes later, not far outside pride lands, Mycroft heard the unmistakable sound of a tire blowing. At the same time, the wheel jerked to the left. Gritting his teeth, he hit the brakes and eased to the shoulder of the road.

"Damn," Dakota muttered. "Blew a tire?"

"Feels like it." Mycroft took a long look around, but they were still in the forest, and he couldn't see much other than trees. With a shake of his head, he unlocked his door and headed outside. "Stay put."

Dakota nodded as he lowered his window, obviously planning to be able to talk to him.

Mycroft reached in and hit the button on the dash to open the back door. Rounding the vehicle, he spotted Forest watching him through the window. The smug smile on the guy's face caused the hairs on his nape to stand on end.

Stopping at the rear blown tire, Mycroft crouched and inspected the tire. He saw a small knife poking out of the sidewall, and it hit him. Jumping to his feet, he hollered, "This wasn't an accident."

Then something stabbed his thigh. He peered down, moving his hand to brush whatever it was away. Except, then the unmistakable feeling of shock flooded his system.

As Mycroft convulsed and dropped to his knees, he finally registered what he'd seen in his leg — prongs to a shock gun.

Seconds later, Mycroft fell to the ground as his eyes rolled to the back of his head.

Mycroft slowly swam to consciousness. He could hear voices, but he couldn't make out the words. Pain ebbed through him, pulsing in waves.

What the fuck happened?

Even as Mycroft wondered that, his memories slammed through him in rapid succession.

Blowing a tire.

Preparing to change it with a spare.

Realizing the tire had been destroyed on purpose.

Getting electrocuted.

Mycroft kept his breathing slow and even, doing his best to feign that he was still asleep. Focusing his thoughts on his time with Boyd kept his scent in check, countering his spike of anxiety. He didn't want his captors to know he was awake.

And just who are my captors?

Forest instantly came to mind, but how could that be? He was in custody. Mycroft prayed that Dakota managed to get away somehow.

Unfortunately, as Mycroft continued to breathe, Dakota's unmistakable scent teased at his nostrils.

Damn.

Forest's sneering voice registered, bringing Mycroft's senses into focus.

"Why the hell did you bring them, Chad?" Forest asked coldly. "You should have just killed them."

"It's a death sentence to kill them," a male voice replied — Chad, evidently. "Besides, we can use them as leverage. Bargaining chips."

Huh. Evidently, Forest isn't the brains of this operation. Shocker.

The sound of flesh hitting flesh reached him.

"You do as I say, Chad," Forest roared. "I'm the alpha."

"Yes, Alpha," Chad replied, a definite whine in his voice. "But, please. We can use them. I promise."

There were several long seconds of silence, and Mycroft mentally prayed to whichever gods cared to listen that the moron believed Chad. He needed time to figure out what to do.

"Fine." The sound of a hand banging on something metal filled the air, and Mycroft felt the ground beneath him jostle. "When are they going to wake up?"

"I'm not certain, Alpha," a second stranger replied. "We had to give them one hell of a jolt to take them down."

"Yeah," Chad agreed. "No way we wanted to deal with that huge Komodo. We don't have the numbers."

The unmistakable scent of fear reached Mycroft's senses.

Excellent. They underestimate me.

"Come on, then," Forest grumbled. "Is everyone here?"

"Yes, Alpha," the stranger answered.

"What kind of weapons did you manage to cobble together?"

Unfortunately, Mycroft wasn't able to distinguish the response.

Mycroft lay there for a moment, counting his breaths and Dakota's breaths, trying to determine if a guard had been left behind.

"Gods, I thought they'd never leave," Dakota whispered, his voice rough with pain. "If I never get hit with electricity again, it'll be too soon."

Easing his eyelids open a crack, Mycroft quickly took in the space. He fought a grimace when he realized they were in a cage . . . and the bars appeared too close together to allow him to slip out, regardless of his shape. Turning his head, Mycroft spotted Dakota lying next to him. The man's eyes were open, but it was clear that his arms were tied behind his back.

"You okay?" Mycroft whispered.

Dakota nodded once. "Yeah. Some bastard got me in the shoulder through the open window," he grumbled, curling his lip. "Have you contacted Boyd about our predicament, yet?"

"Contacted Boyd?" Mycroft repeated in confusion.

Dakota nodded once. "Yeah." His brows furrowed for a second before he arched one brow and pinned him with a sardonic smile. "You're bonded with a vampire. You can speak telepathically."

"Shit," Mycroft hissed. "I totally forgot about that." Scoffing, he admitted, "We haven't tried it, yet."

Scoffing, Dakota quipped, "Well, now might be a real good time for you to start practicing." After that, he rolled so his back was to Mycroft. "You mind unlocking me?"

Mycroft spotted the cuffs on Dakota's wrists—the special ones they'd brought—and he nodded. "Yup." He glanced toward the hall where the others had obviously gone, then eased to his knees and crawled over to Dakota.

One of the things every enforcer was taught to do was to pick the cuffs. That was why they affixed them behind the shifter's back. A shifter couldn't pick them if they couldn't see them.

Carefully, Mycroft shifted his fingers to claws. Then he eased the claw of each forepaw into the slot to work them. As he concentrated on that, Mycroft reached out with his mind and called to Boyd.

CHAPTER TEN

B*oyd?*
Lifting his head from the box he was packing, Boyd glanced around the room. He frowned, not seeing anyone. He headed to the doorway and paused in the frame, sweeping his gaze over his front room.

"Did you call for me?" Boyd asked Murdoch, who was busy clearing out his refrigerator.

Murdoch straightened and peered his way. "No," he replied, sounding confused.

Boyd? Can you hear me?

"There it is again," Boyd exclaimed.

"There *what* is?"

Frowning, Boyd asked, "You don't hear that? Someone calling my name?"

Shaking his head, Murdoch grinned. "You hearing voices, now, Boyd?" Then his buddy's eyes widened. "Could it be Mycroft?"

Boyd scoffed. "I think I would have recognized my phone's ringtone."

Murdoch rolled his eyes. "Not on your phone, dumbass," he teased. Then he touched his temple. "Through your bond. In your head."

"Oh, shit." Boyd barked a laugh as he grinned at Murdoch. "I totally forgot about that. We hadn't even tried to talk telepathically, yet."

"Well, maybe that's what Mycroft is trying to do," Murdoch offered. "Give it a go. Try talking back to him."

Leaning against the doorframe, Boyd reached out with his mind. *Mycroft? Is that you?*

Boyd! Thank the gods.

My beloved. It is you. Boyd grinned and gave a thumbs up to Murdoch, who laughed and returned to cleaning out his fridge. *What's up? Are you almost here?*

I'm afraid we ran into a bit of a hiccup. Mycroft's frustration bled through their bond. *Some moronic followers of Forest blew out our tire, kidnapped us, and rescued Forest.*

"What?" Boyd roared, forgetting to speak through his mind.

Murdoch immediately jerked to face him. "What is it?"

"Find the master," Boyd demanded. "My beloved has been kidnapped, and Forest is loose."

"Damn it." A second later, Murdoch rushed from the room.

Where are you? Boyd asked Mycroft, gripping the doorframe. His claws slid out, scoring the wood. *Are you injured? Are you okay?*

Unfortunately, I don't know where I am. Mycroft sounded a little distracted. *Dakota and I are in a cage. They put our cuffs on him.* His beloved scoffed. *Evidently, they were worried about meeting his Komodo dragon, so some of them must have been at the challenge. Bradley told me that a couple of them left as opposed to accepting him as alpha, so I imagine they're around here somewhere.*

Got it. Satisfaction flooded their link. *We were only about thirty minutes from the main cougar house, so we can't be too far from there.*

Can you tell me anything? Boyd did his best to keep his desperation from bleeding through. *Give me some way to find you?*

I'm sorry, my mate.

Boyd was at a loss, struggling with something to say.

Then Mycroft reached out again. *We're breaking out of the cage. There's a window. We're going to look out and see if we can spot a landmark or something.*

"I got the location of the SUV," Mathe stated, striding into the room behind Master Jaymes. The ranch foreman was holding a tablet, tapping on it with his other hand. "Come on. We can be there in fifteen minutes if we speed."

We're on our way to the SUV. It's got a tracker on it. Boyd relayed the information as he rushed from the room with the others. *We'll find you. Just stay safe.*

I'll do my best. Oh. Nice. Mycroft sounded amused. *They changed the blown tire on the SUV. It's parked right outside. Guess we'll see you soon.*

Perfect.

Oops. Going out the window. Mycroft sounded distracted again. *We're going to hide in the woods. Be careful, my mate.*

The next fifteen minutes were the longest of Boyd's life. He drummed his fingers on the door handle. His foot tapped against the floor, and he couldn't seem to control it.

Boyd was in the first of three vehicles full of vampires barreling down the road toward his beloved. Every moment, Boyd feared he would hear something through his link that would mean his beloved was in danger. Over and over, he barely resisted the urge to contact Mycroft. He didn't want to distract his shifter if he was in the middle of something.

"Take a few deep breaths," Master Jaymes urged, touching Boyd's shoulder. "Calm yourself. Have faith in your beloved."

Nodding, Boyd did as his master bid. He focused on breathing slowly, taking one deep breath at a time. He reminded himself that Mycroft was not just an enforcer but the head enforcer of the damn shifter council. Boyd had to believe that his shifter could protect himself.

"So much better, Boyd," Jaymes rumbled, continuing to rub his neck. "Your Mycroft is a strong shifter. Powerful in his own right. Have faith in him," he encouraged. "Have faith in your bond. He has a reason to be careful. He'll come back to you."

Boyd nodded again, hanging onto his master's words with every fiber of his being.

When they arrived on scene, they drove into chaos. Cougars and men were running in all directions. The men held guns as they scoured the grounds. The cougars were sniffing at bushes and leaping between tree branches.

The fact that they were searching for something was beyond obvious.

The man standing on the porch of the rundown cabin was shouting obscenities at everyone, the words easy to hear even over the rumble of the SUV's engine.

When the noise shut off, the guy was hollering, "You gods damned morons. I told you we should have killed them." He smacked the nearest man upside the head, sending him stumbling off the porch. "Find them!"

"Yes, Alpha Forest," the man bent at his waist in obeyance, tilting his head to the side. "We'll find them. We won't fail you again."

When Master Jaymes exited the vehicle, Boyd followed suit.

"Forest," Jaymes called, striding forward slowly, his second and enforcers converging around him. He indicated the black vehicle they'd parked beside. "Why have you stolen one of my coven's SUVs?"

The nearly dozen shifters began to creep closer, converging on the vampires. They glanced between each other, their movements wary.

"That's *Alpha* Forest," the shifter responded belligerently. Crossing his arms over his chest, he claimed, "And this vehicle was being driven by a rogue. He must have been the one who stole it."

"This vehicle was being driven by my beloved," Boyd shouted, anger coursing through him. His vision began to haze, allowing him to map the beat of everyone's hearts as it pumped their blood through their systems. There were a lot of nervous shifters in the area. "You dared to touch the bonded beloved of a vampire in this coven."

"That's a declaration of war, Forest," Master Jaymes pointed out, his tone taking on a bored note. "Return those in the SUV, and I may think about sparing your people."

"I'm Alpha Forest," the unhinged man screamed. "And you'll never see that shifter again." Pointing, he bellowed, "Kill them all!"

For an instant, all the shifters seemed frozen, as if they didn't understand the order.

Then they reacted. Some turned and streaked into the forest, clearly fleeing. Others obeyed, leaping at the closest vampire or firing their weapons at them.

Boyd pivoted out of the way of an attacking cougar. With a swing of his arm, he raked his talons along the beast's side. Blood spurted, coating the ground where the shifter fell and didn't get up.

A huge lizard appeared from the trees, clamping its jaws around one fleeing between tree trunks.

Too busy gaping at what had to be Dakota in Komodo dragon form, Boyd nearly missed the fact that some shifter was pointing a gun at him.

Gypsum shoved Boyd forward, then converged on the shifter. "Eyes up, Boyd," he rumbled before using his talons to lop off the shifter's head.

Boyd nodded. "Thanks." Then he sprinted to the left and engaged another shifter in cougar form.

"Cowards," Forest roared. Except, then he attempted to follow those who'd disappeared into the forest.

Just as Boyd was turning, intending to give chase—no way did he want that bastard to get away—a gorgeous cheetah shot from between bushes, intercepting Forest. Forest curled his lip as he eyed what had to be Mycroft in cheetah form. He had his lips curved way from his eye-teeth, and he snarled in warning at the ex-alpha.

For one heartbeat, two, Forest stared at the cheetah. Then he began to shift.

To Boyd's shock, Mycroft sat down and watched Forest change. If he had to guess, he saw disdain on the feline's features.

"What the hell is he doing?" Mathe asked, sounding shocked, expressing Boyd's thoughts exactly.

Relax, my mate. Even in cat form, Mycroft's thoughts reached Boyd. *It's time to put an end to this cougar, and it must be done in the proper way.*

Proper way? Boyd couldn't believe what he was hearing.

Yes. Trust me, my mate. Mycroft flicked an ear as he glanced his way for just an instant. *Keep your people back.*

Spotting movement to the right, Boyd saw several vampire trackers creeping toward Forest, who was just finishing his shift. "Stay back," Boyd ordered, lifting a hand in warning. "Mycroft says not to interfere."

"Do as Boyd says," Master Jaymes called, reinforcing the command.

After a glance at their master, the vampires relaxed and took several steps backward.

As soon as Forest finished shifting, he lunged at Mycroft. Instead of jumping away, his cheetah flopped to the left and rolled, causing Forest to miss. Mycroft was back on his haunches in a flash, and he streaked toward a still running Forest.

The ex-alpha was obviously making a break for it.

Mycroft raced past Forest's backside, taking out his rear legs with a swipe of his paw. Jumping, he planted his paws on a tree trunk and pushed off, reversing directions. Twisting in midair, Mycroft landed on a rising Forest's back, taking him back to the ground.

Wrapping his jaws around Forest's throat, Mycroft jerked his head, tearing it out. His cheetah stood, spitting out the cougar's flesh. He prowled around the downed cougar, growling, watching as the light dimmed and finally went out.

Forest was dead.

With a soft chuff, Mycroft turned away from the downed cougar. He padded toward Boyd, his head high and his green eyes gleaming. Stopping beside Boyd, Mycroft rubbed his head against his hip, rowling softly in greeting.

Boyd let out a deep sigh as he rubbed his fingers through his beloved's fur, scratching his ears and earning him pleased rumbles.

"Damn, my beloved," Boyd whispered, crouching before his cheetah. "You scared the ever-loving shit out of me."

Mycroft rumbled softly, the noise sounding suspiciously like an apology. Then, beneath his palms, his beloved began to shift.

Quickly shucking his shirt, Boyd offered it to his lover. His shifter chuckled, but he took it without question. He wrapped it around his waist, using the arms to tie it on.

Then Boyd wrapped his arms around Mycroft and clutched him close.

"I'm sorry for scaring you, Boyd," Mycroft murmured, nuzzling his temple against Boyd's, just as if he were still in cat form. "Try to remember, this is what I'm trained for. He was no match for me."

Issuing a deep sigh, Boyd nodded. "I understand." He lifted his head and peered into Mycroft's warm gaze. "Our relationship is new, still developing" — smirking, he added — "even if it is going at cheetah speed." Cradling Mycroft's jaw, Boyd told him, "I'll catch up. It'll just take a little time. That's all."

Mycroft smiled widely. "I'll give you all the time you need, my mate."

"Thank you." Boyd grinned back. "And I look forward to exploring all that time with you."

Before Mycroft could respond, Dakota's deep voice called, "Don't worry, boss-man. None of the ones who fled escaped." A low chuckle erupted from the large . . . naked . . . man, as he strolled from between the trees. "They all got what they deserved."

Mycroft snorted as he rolled his eyes. "Well done, Dakota." Arching one brow, he asked, "Can someone loan the guy a shirt or something?"

"I don't know," Clarice purred even as one of the male vampires whipped his shirt over his head and tossed it to Dakota. "I'm rather enjoying the view."

With the shirt in hand, Dakota lifted both arms and flexed, taking on a bodybuilder pose.

Groaning, Mycroft used his arm around Boyd to turn them away from the sight. "Let's go, my mate," he urged. "We have a move to finish."

"That we do." Boyd couldn't remember looking forward to anything more.

ABOUT THE AUTHOR

Charlie started writing fantasy when she was eight, and after stumbling onto her first erotic romance at age nineteen, she realized her true calling. She now focuses on writing gay erotic romance, normally of the paranormal variety, with heroes of all kinds. With the help and support of her husband, Charlie finally fulfilled one of her life-long goals . . . move to acreage with her horses. You can often find her curled up with her laptop and a cup of tea or glass of wine, creating her next adventure. Charlie enjoys exploring the mountains of her new Oregon home on horseback, 4-wheeler, or motorcycle.

She can be reached at ch.richards2010@yahoo.com

Or visit her at www.charlie-richards.com.

www.ingramcontent.com/pod-product-compliance
Lightning Source LLC
Chambersburg PA
CBHW070538130626
46555CB00003B/1484